HAVE YOU READ THESE NARWHAL AND JELLY BOOKS?

NARWHAL: UNICORN OF THE SEA!

SUPER NARWHAL AND JELLY JOLT

PEANUT
BUTTER
AND JELLY

BEN CLANTON

tundra

FOR ALEX COX!
KEEP SPREADING THE AWESOMENESS!

Text and illustrations copyright © 2018 by Ben Clanton

Tundra Books, an imprint of Penguin Random House Canada Young Readers, a Penguin Random House Company

Library and Archives Canada Cataloguing in Publication

Clanton, Ben, 1988-, author
Peanut butter and Jelly / Ben Clanton.
(A Narwhal and Jelly book)
Issued in print and electronic formats.
ISBN 978-0-7352-6245-4 (hardcover).—ISBN 978-0-7352-6247-8 (epub)

1. Graphic novels. I. Title.

PZ7.7.C53Pea 2017   j741.5'973   C2017-902644-5
                                                         C2017-902645-3

Published simultaneously in the United States of America by Tundra Books of Northern New York, an imprint of Penguin Random House Canada Young Readers, a Penguin Random House Company

Library of Congress Control Number: 2017939300

Edited by Tara Walker and Jessica Burgess
Designed by Ben Clanton and Andrew Roberts

The artwork in this book was rendered in colored pencil, watercolor and ink, and colored digitally.
The text was handlettered by Ben Clanton.

Photos: (waffle) © Tiger Images/Shutterstock; (strawberry) © Valentina Razumova/Shutterstock; (pickle) © dominitsky/Shutterstock; (boom box) © valio84sl/Thinkstock; (jars) © choness/Thinkstock; (peanuts) © Zoonar/homydesign/Thinkstock; (jam on bread) © George Doyle/Thinkstock; (peanut butter toast) © NicholasBPhotography/Thinkstock

Printed and bound in China

www.penguinrandomhouse.ca

1 2 3 4 5   22 21 20 19 18

CONTENTS

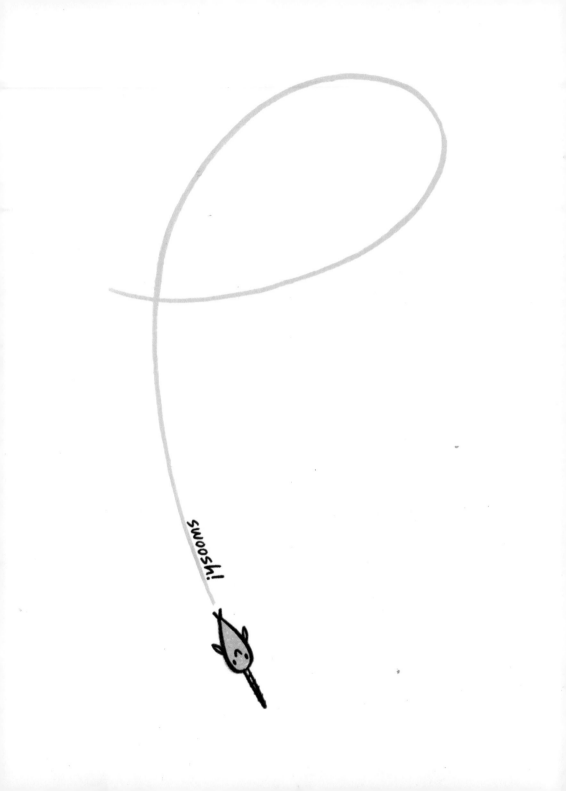

swoosh!

A SWEET
AND SALTY
STORY!

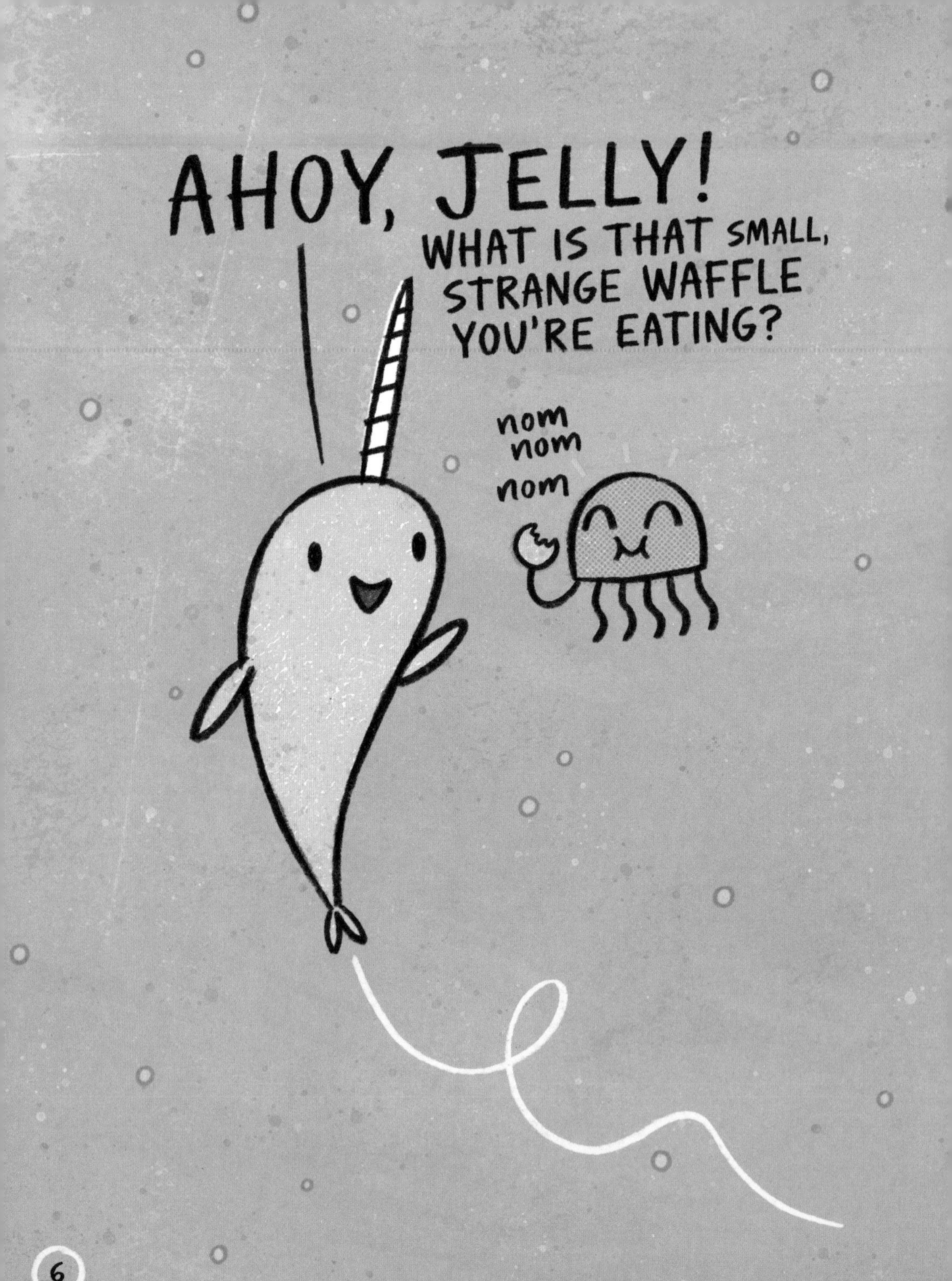
AHOY, JELLY!
WHAT IS THAT SMALL, STRANGE WAFFLE YOU'RE EATING?
nom nom nom

UM...NARWHAL,
THIS IS **NOT** A WAFFLE.
IT IS A PEANUT BUTTER
COOKIE.

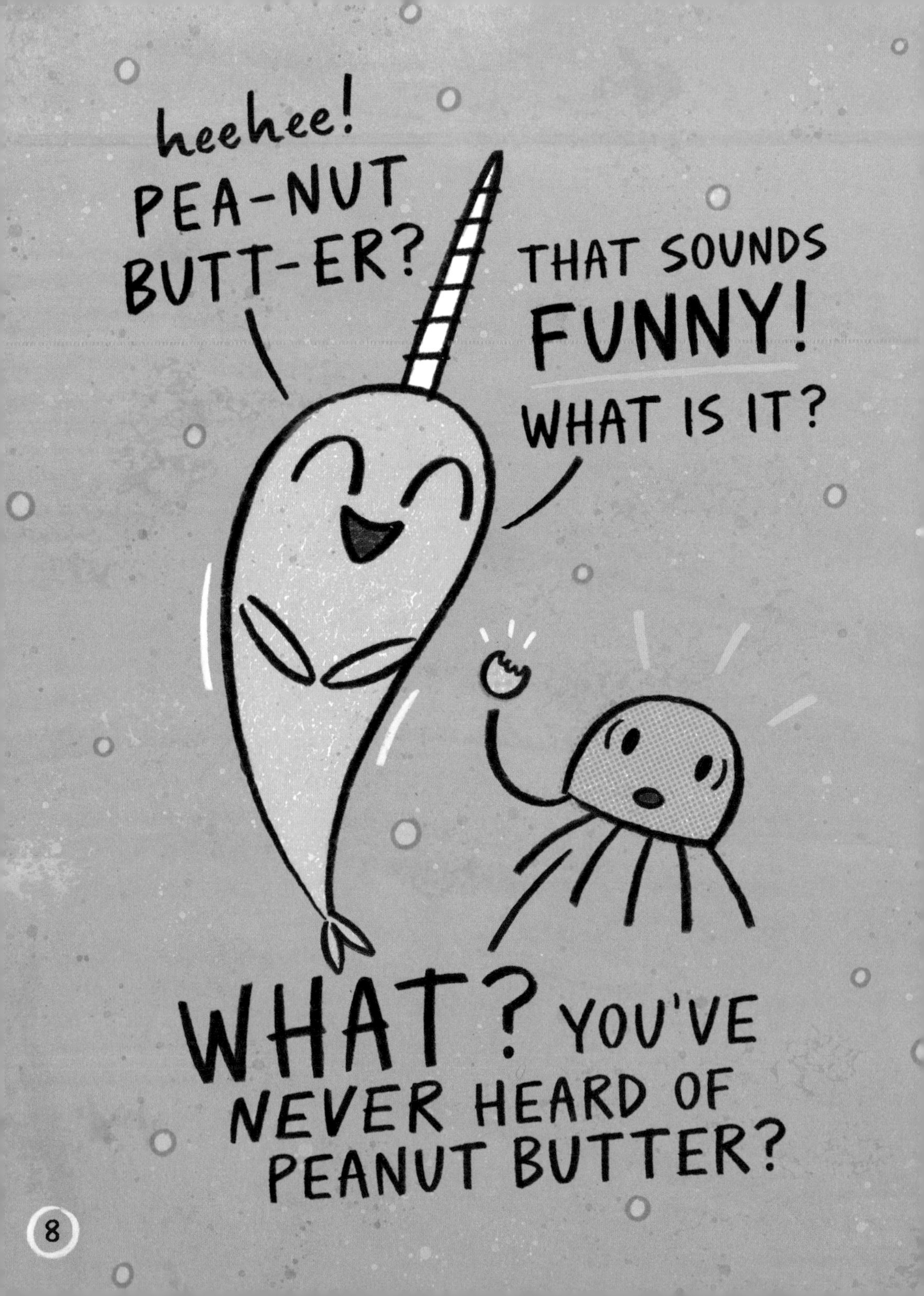
heehee!
PEA-NUT BUTT-ER?
THAT SOUNDS FUNNY!
WHAT IS IT?
WHAT? YOU'VE NEVER HEARD OF PEANUT BUTTER?

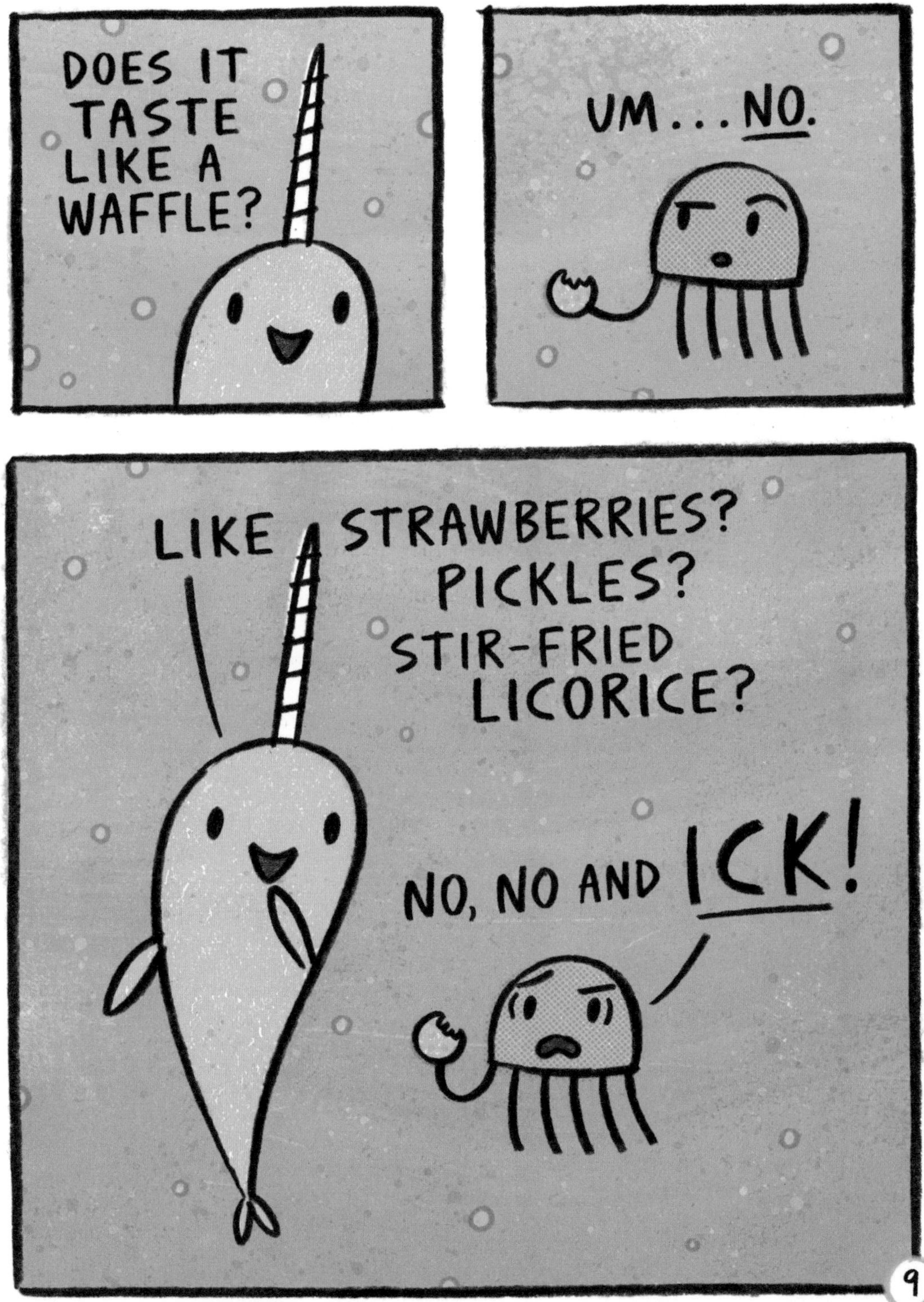
DOES IT TASTE LIKE A WAFFLE?
UM... NO.
LIKE STRAWBERRIES? PICKLES? STIR-FRIED LICORICE?
NO, NO AND ICK!

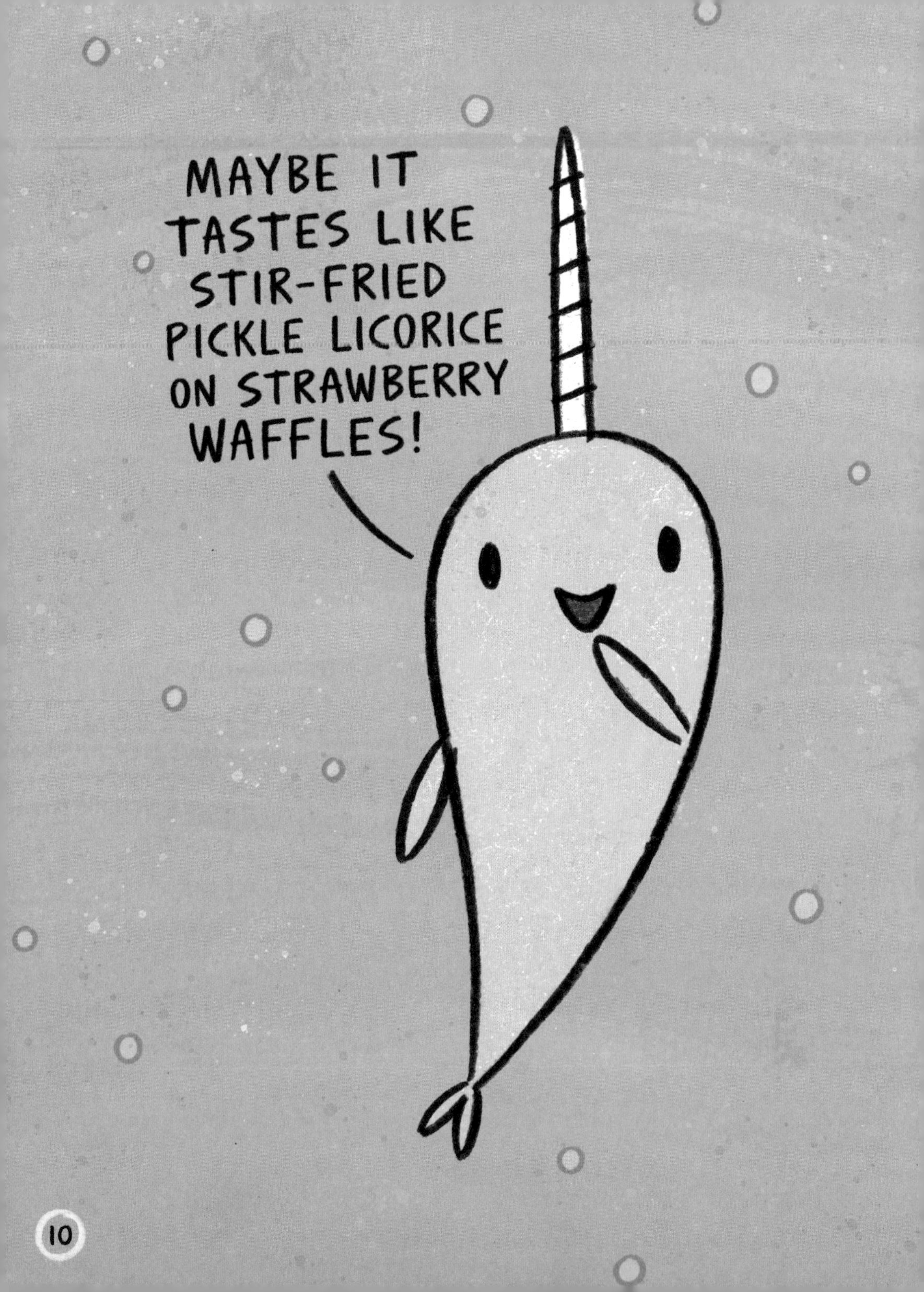
MAYBE IT TASTES LIKE STIR-FRIED PICKLE LICORICE ON STRAWBERRY WAFFLES!

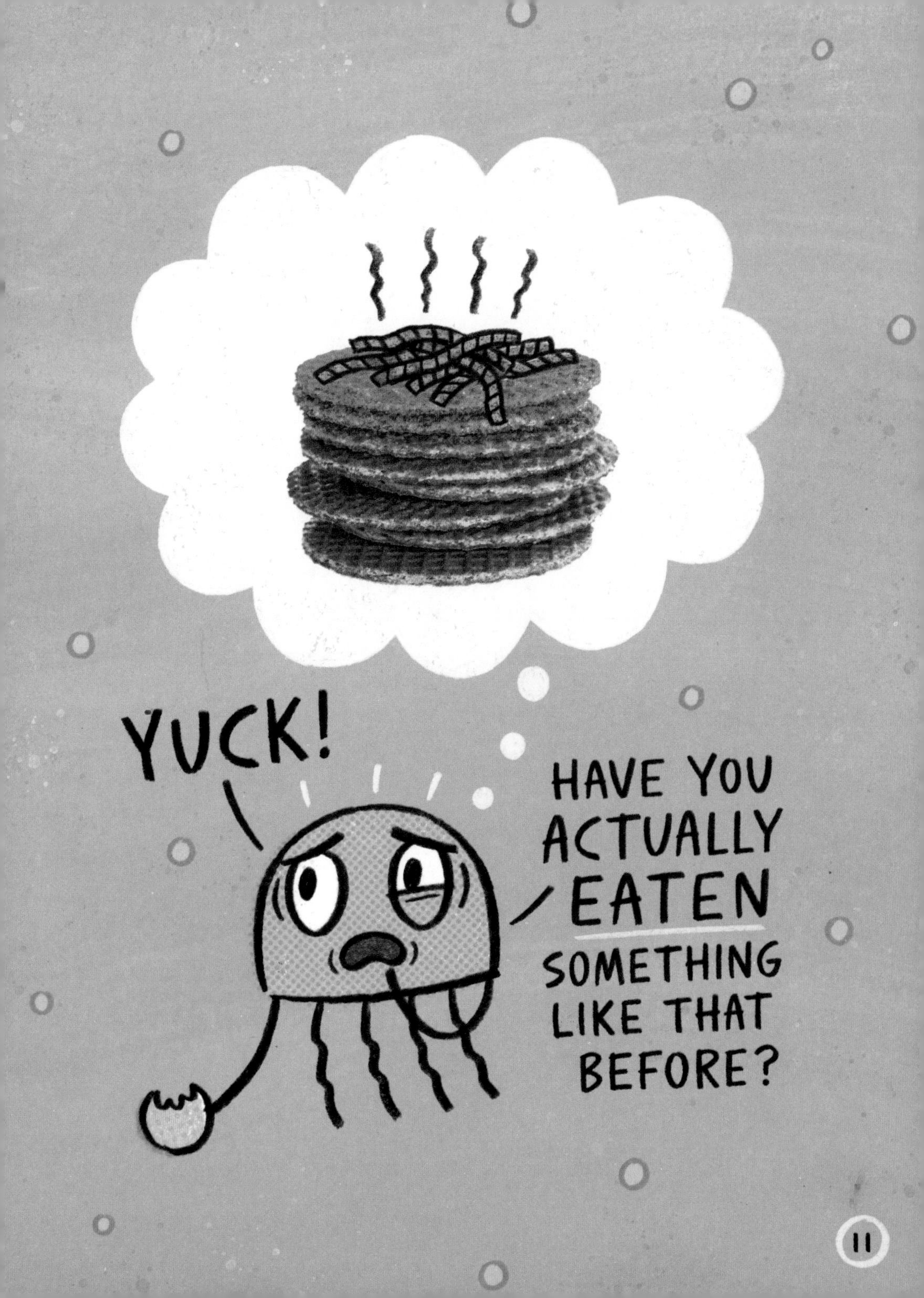
YUCK!
HAVE YOU ACTUALLY EATEN SOMETHING LIKE THAT BEFORE?

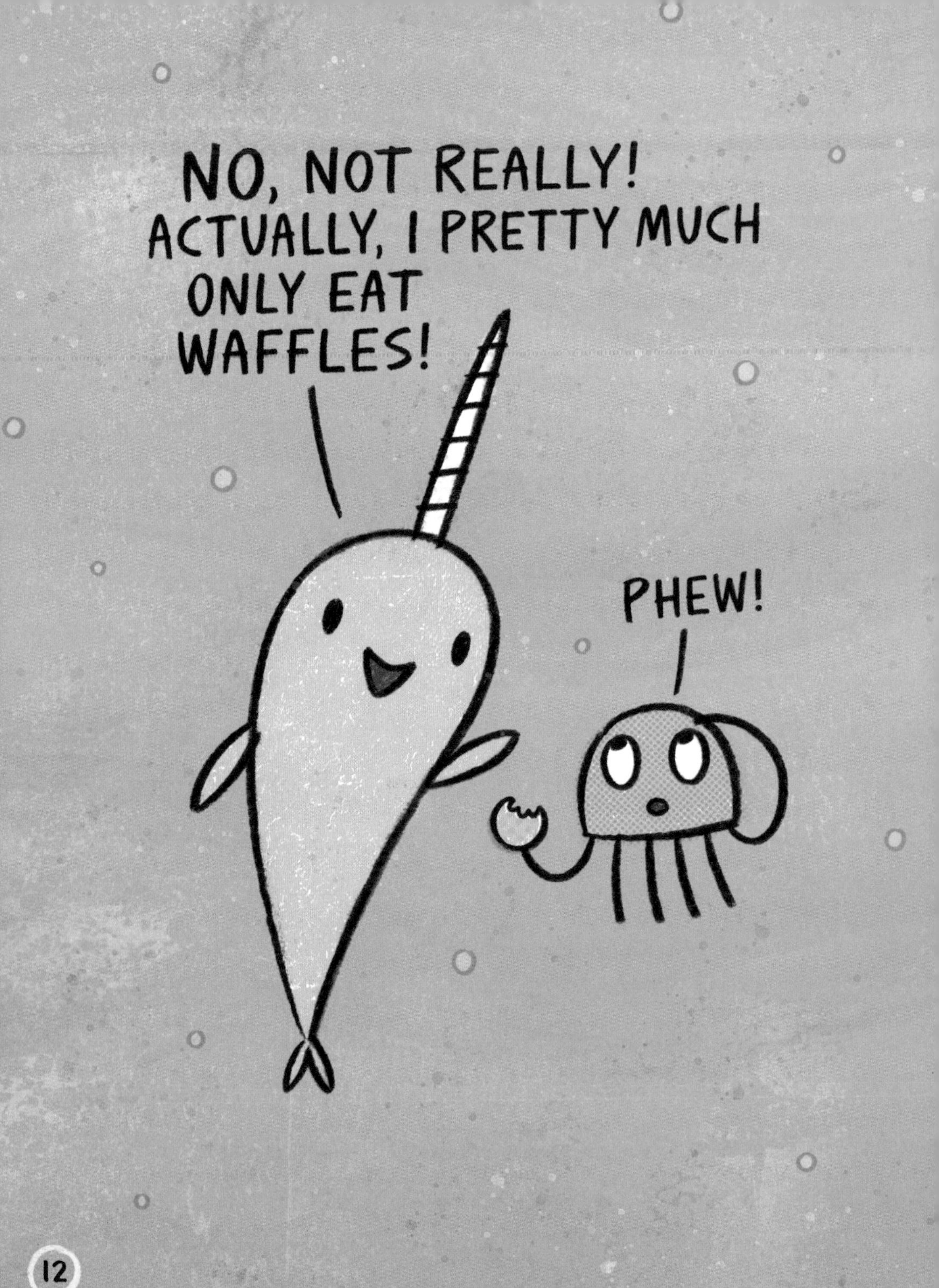
NO, NOT REALLY! ACTUALLY, I PRETTY MUCH ONLY EAT WAFFLES!
PHEW!

WAIT A MINUTE...
ONLY WAFFLES?

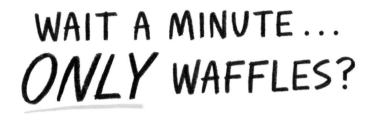

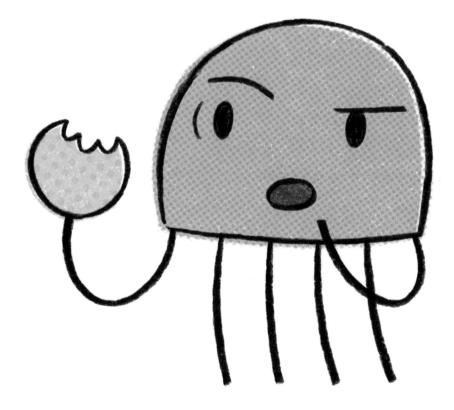

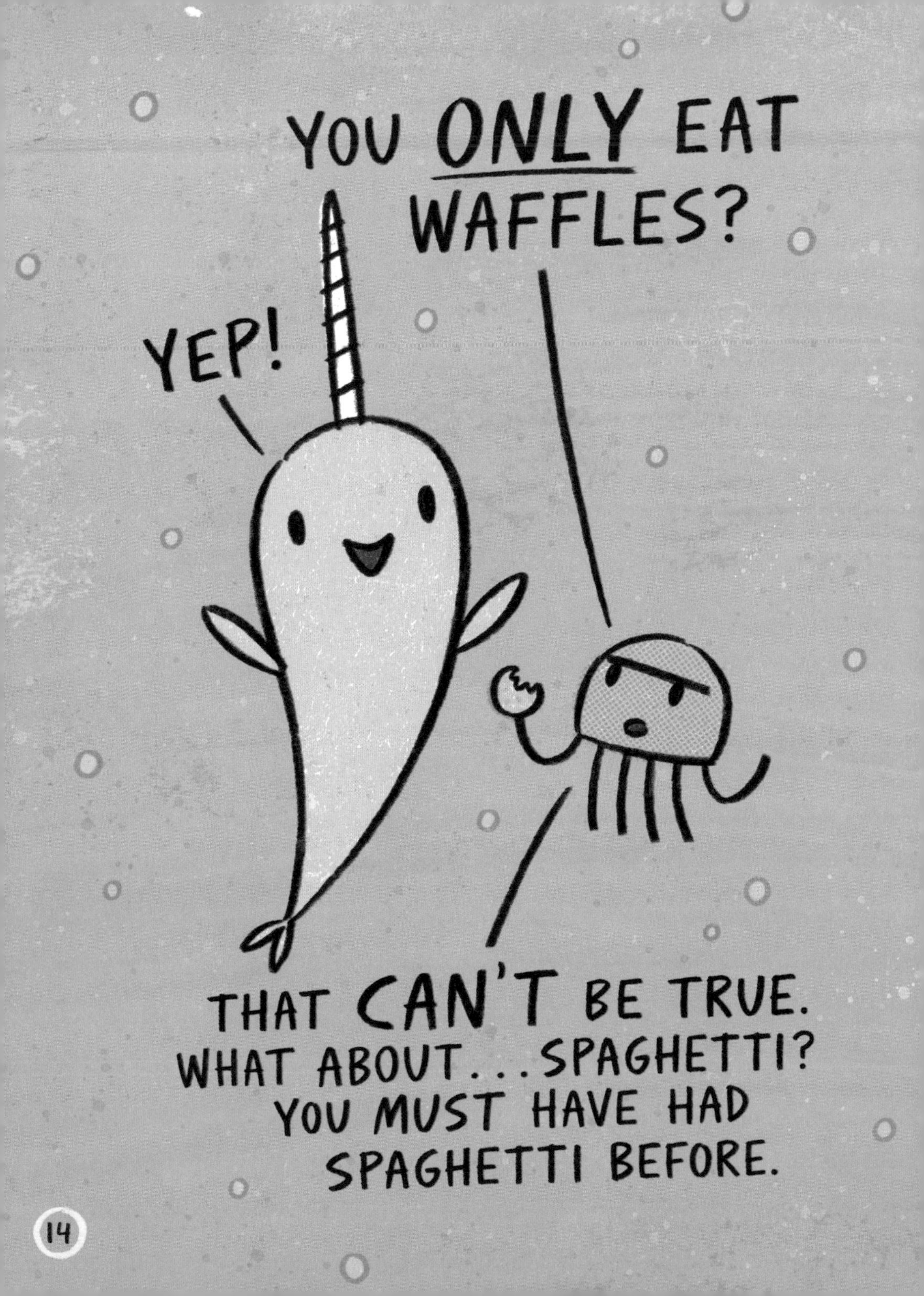

YOU ONLY EAT WAFFLES?
YEP!
THAT CAN'T BE TRUE. WHAT ABOUT...SPAGHETTI? YOU MUST HAVE HAD SPAGHETTI BEFORE.

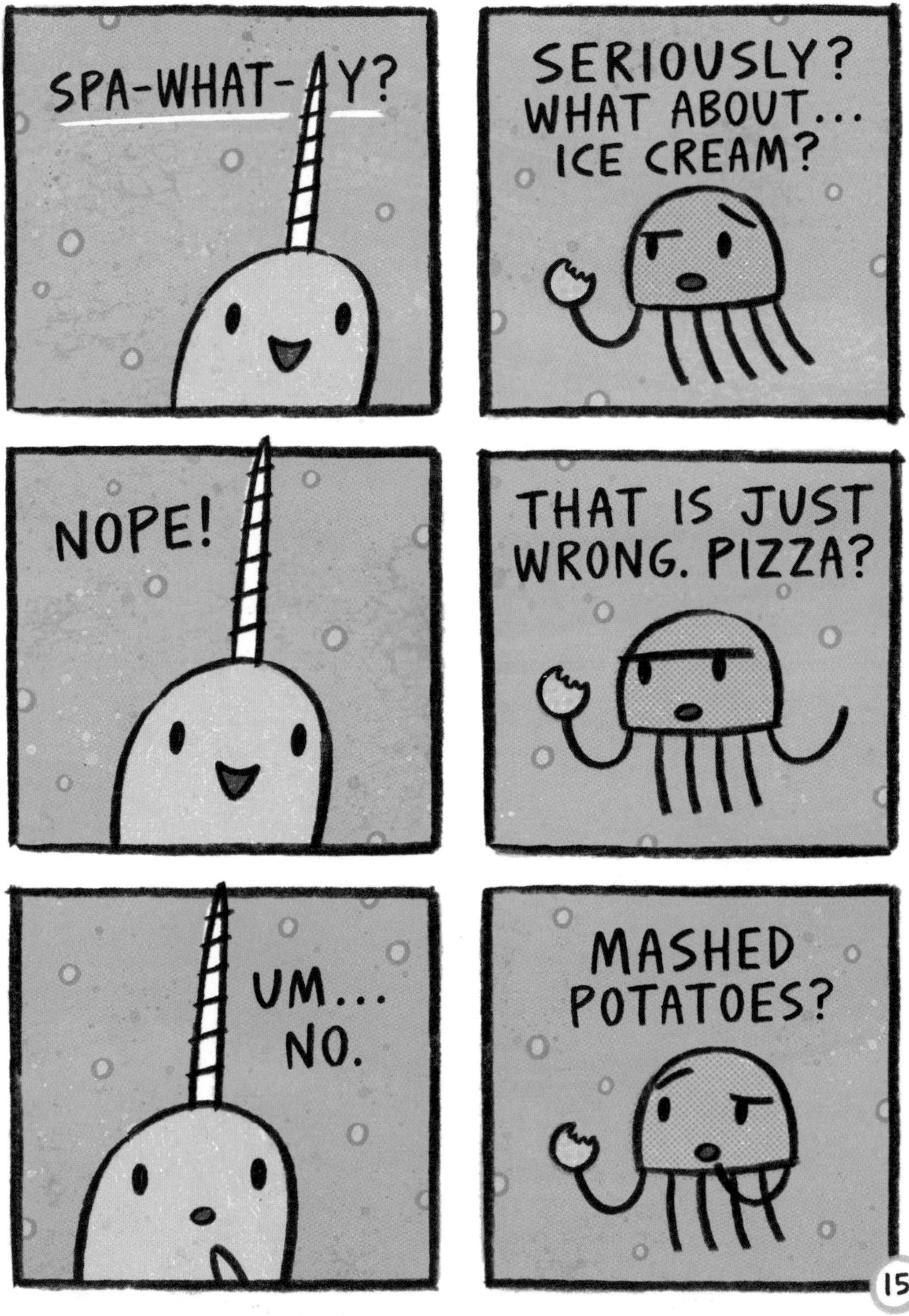
SPA-WHAT-Y?
SERIOUSLY? WHAT ABOUT... ICE CREAM?
NOPE!
THAT IS JUST WRONG. PIZZA?
UM... NO.
MASHED POTATOES?

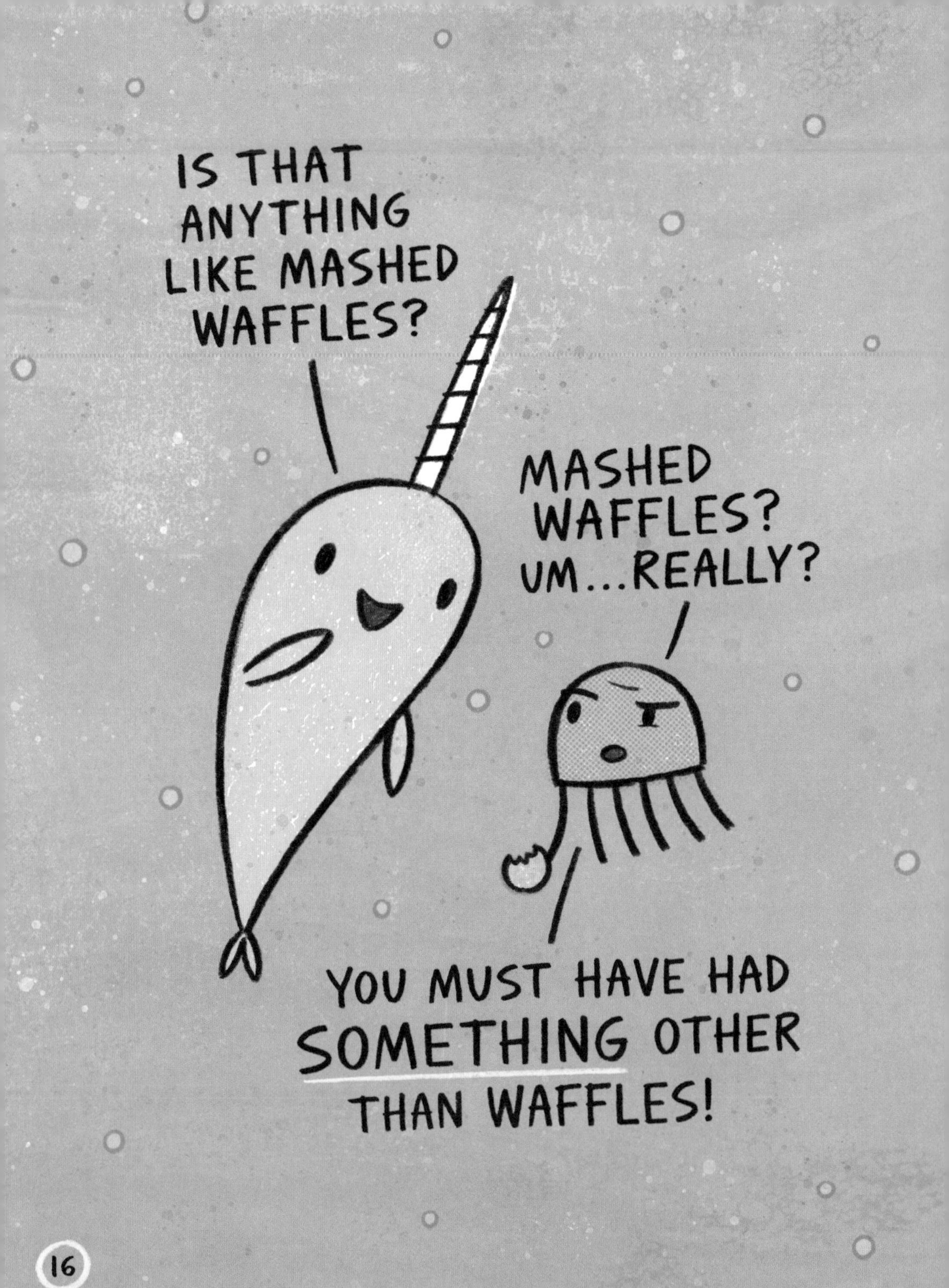
IS THAT ANYTHING LIKE MASHED WAFFLES?
MASHED WAFFLES? UM...REALLY?
YOU MUST HAVE HAD SOMETHING OTHER THAN WAFFLES!

CAKE? APPLES?
CHEESE? PIE?
ARTICHOKES?
MARSHMALLOWS?
GUACAMOLE?
UH…SUSHI?
FRENCH FRIES?

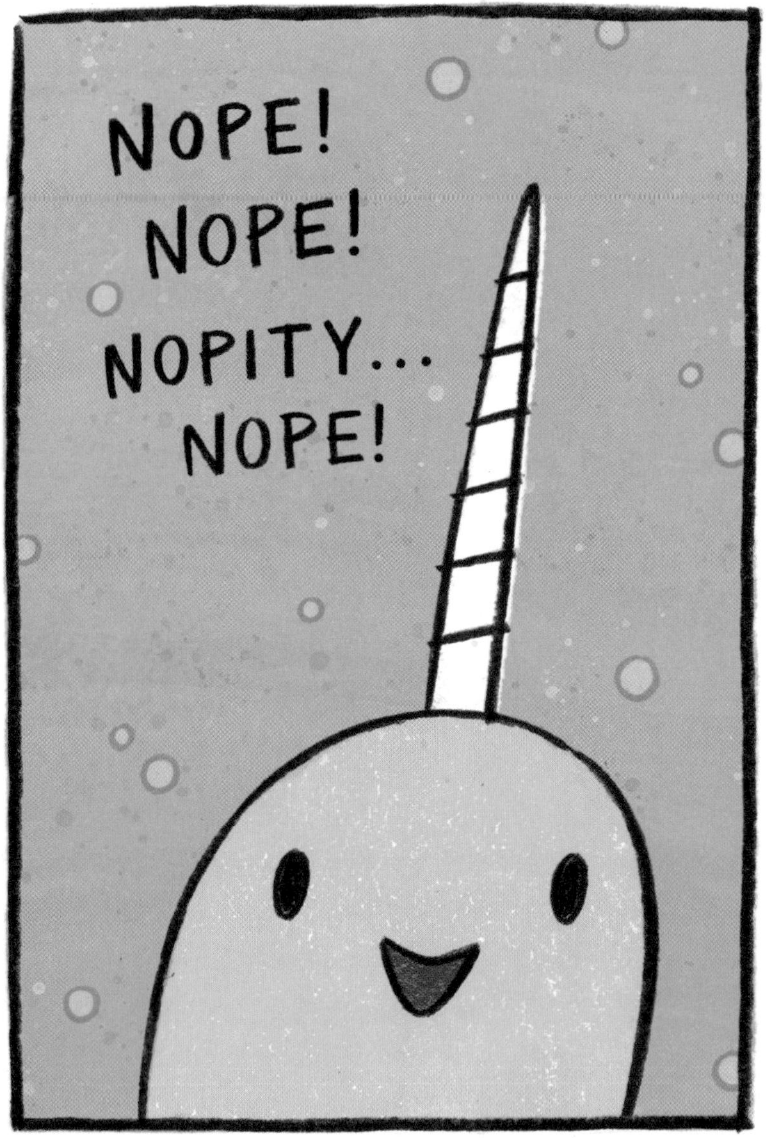
NOPE!
NOPE!
NOPITY...
NOPE!

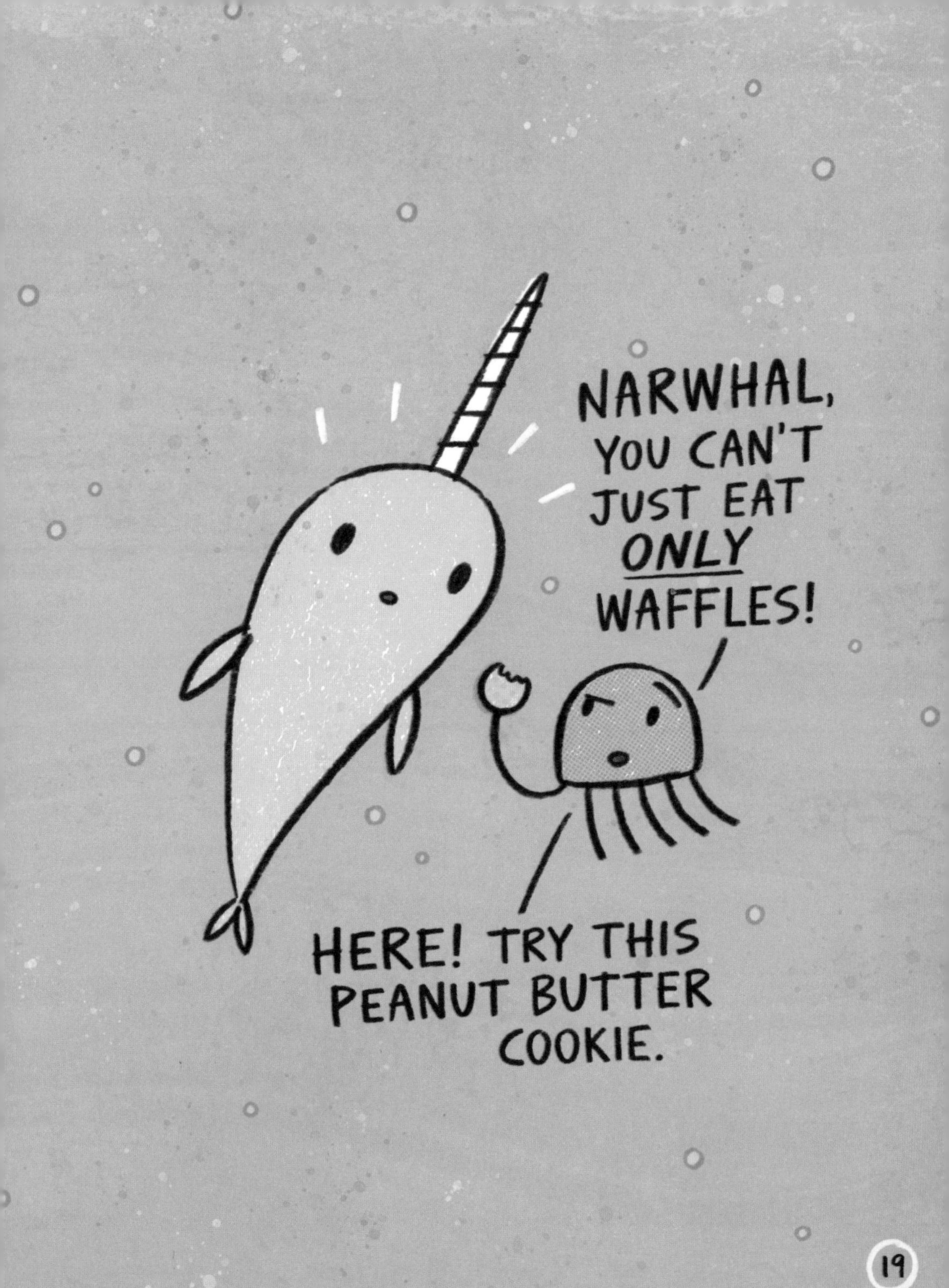
NARWHAL, YOU CAN'T JUST EAT ONLY WAFFLES!
HERE! TRY THIS PEANUT BUTTER COOKIE.

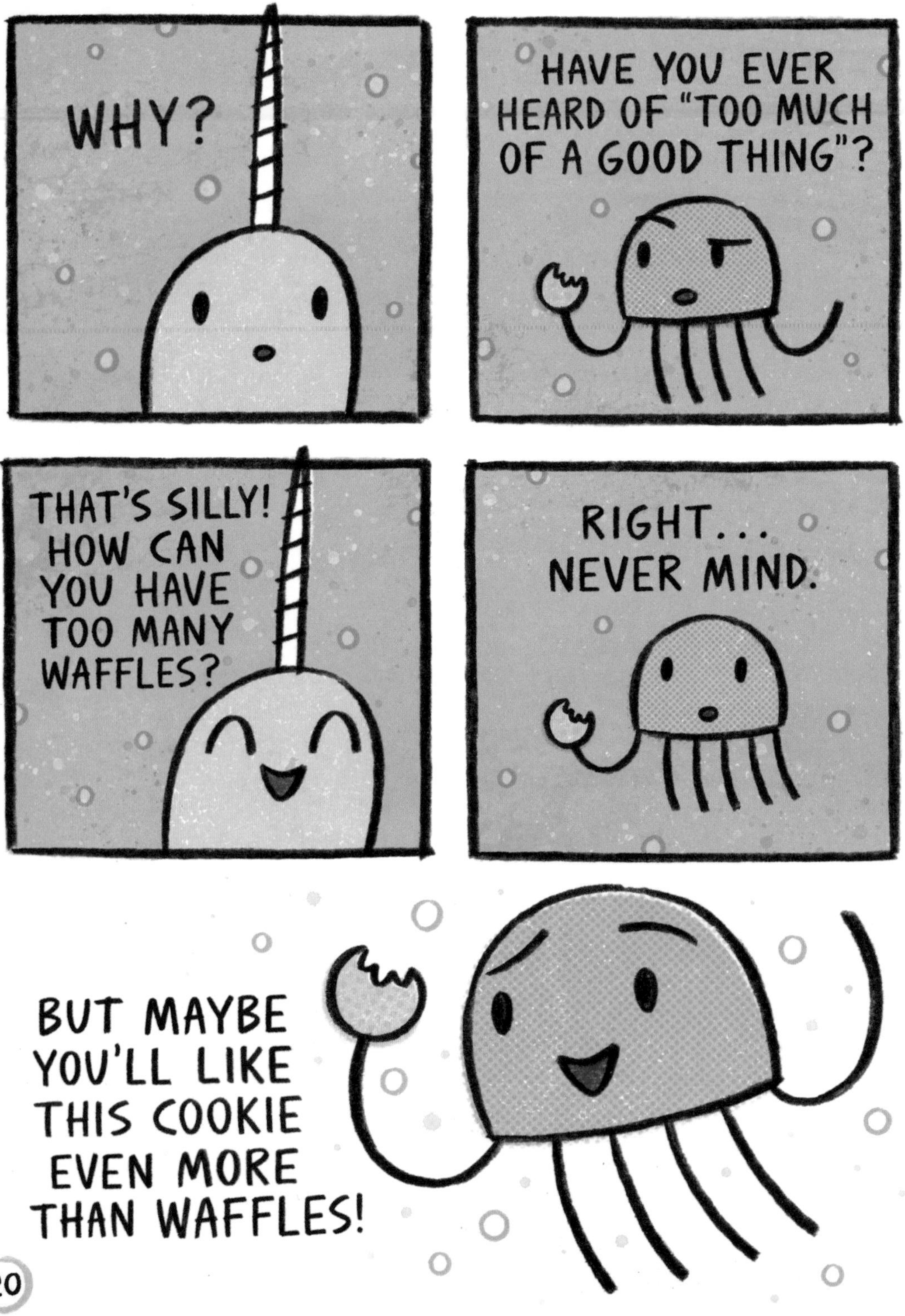
WHY?
HAVE YOU EVER HEARD OF "TOO MUCH OF A GOOD THING"?
THAT'S SILLY! HOW CAN YOU HAVE TOO MANY WAFFLES?
RIGHT... NEVER MIND.
BUT MAYBE YOU'LL LIKE THIS COOKIE EVEN MORE THAN WAFFLES!

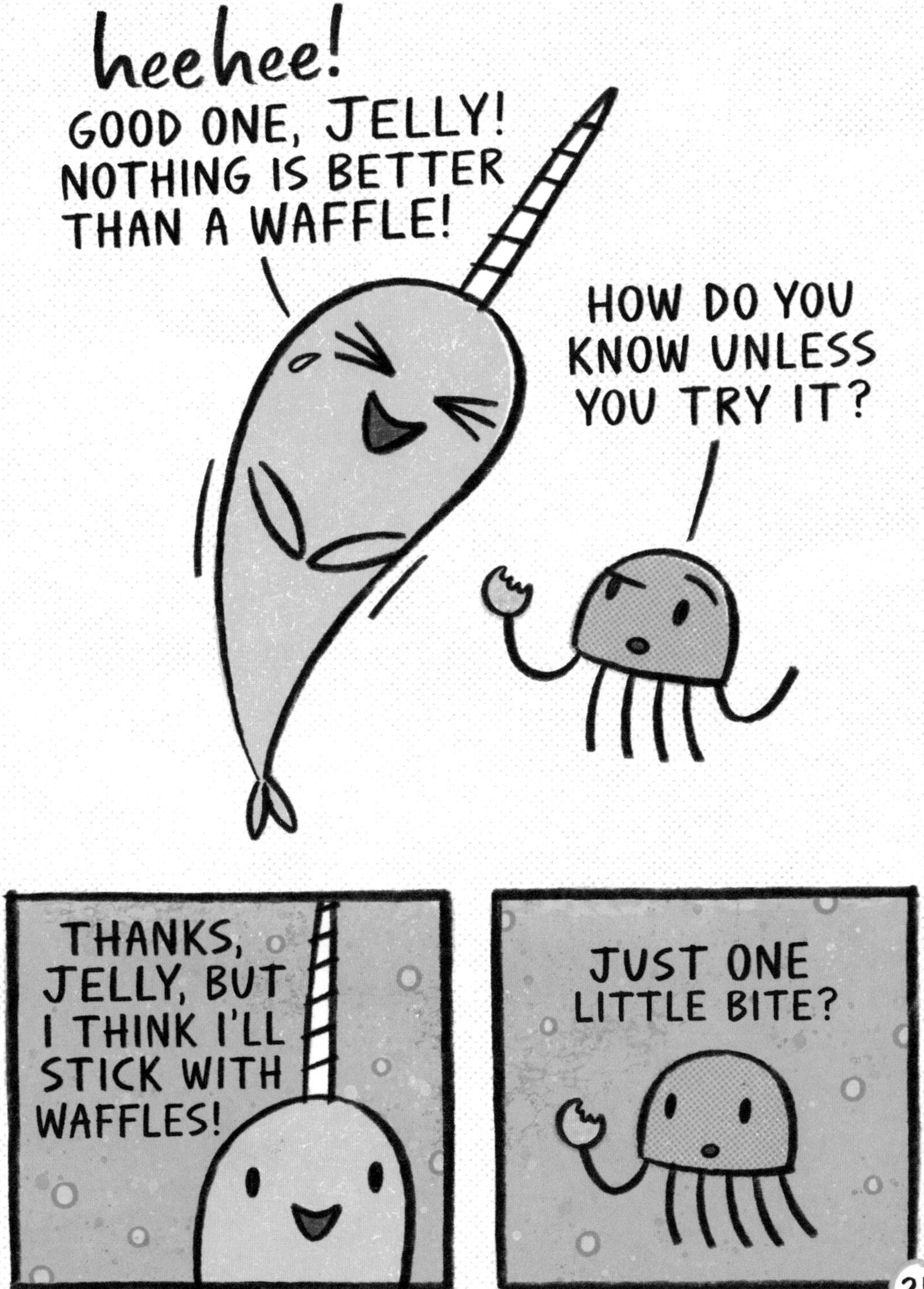
heehee!
GOOD ONE, JELLY! NOTHING IS BETTER THAN A WAFFLE!
HOW DO YOU KNOW UNLESS YOU TRY IT?
THANKS, JELLY, BUT I THINK I'LL STICK WITH WAFFLES!
JUST ONE LITTLE BITE?

I TELL YOU WHAT, I'LL MAKE YOU AN **EXTRA LARGE** WAFFLE IF YOU JUST TRY THIS PEANUT BUTTER COOKIE.

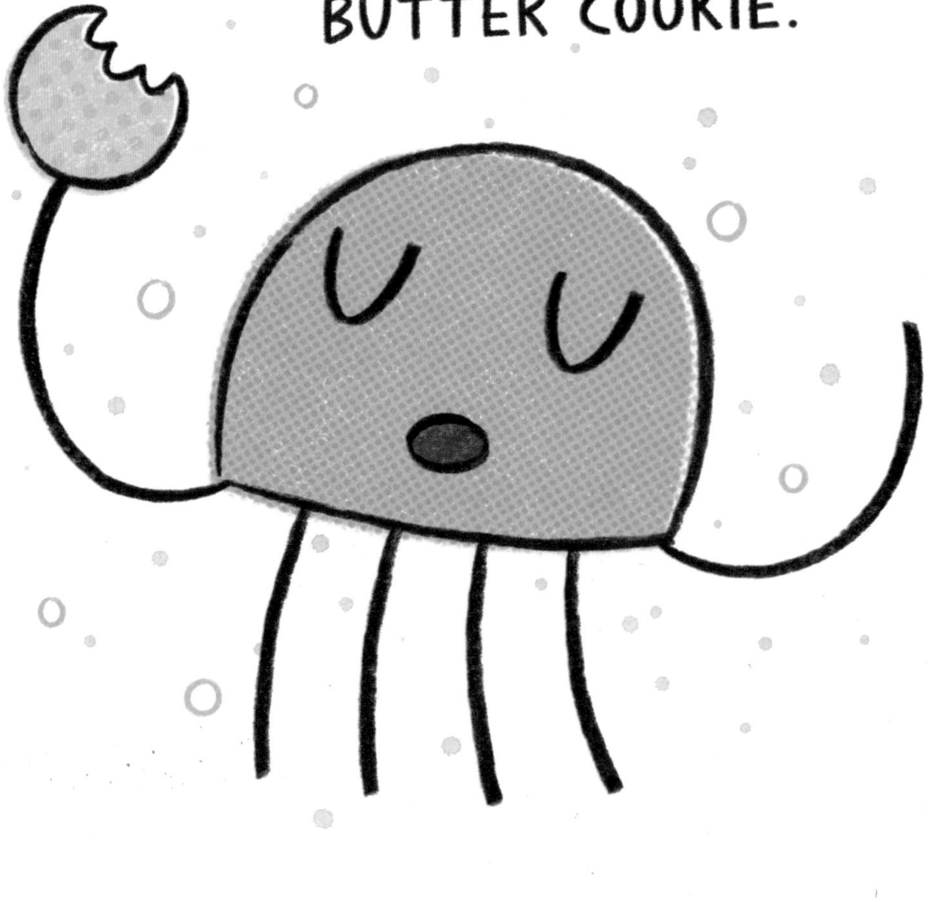

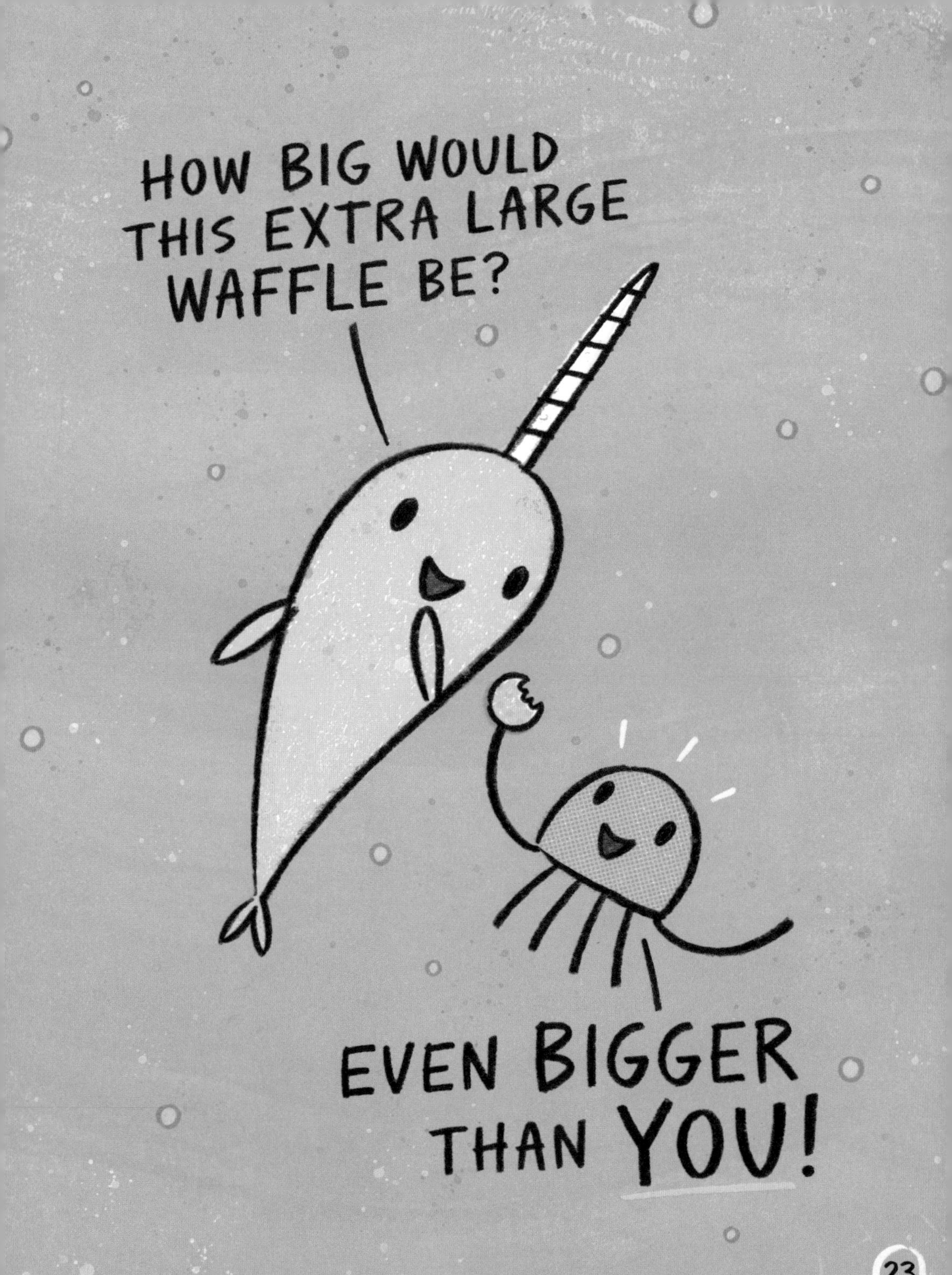
HOW BIG WOULD THIS EXTRA LARGE WAFFLE BE?
EVEN BIGGER THAN YOU!

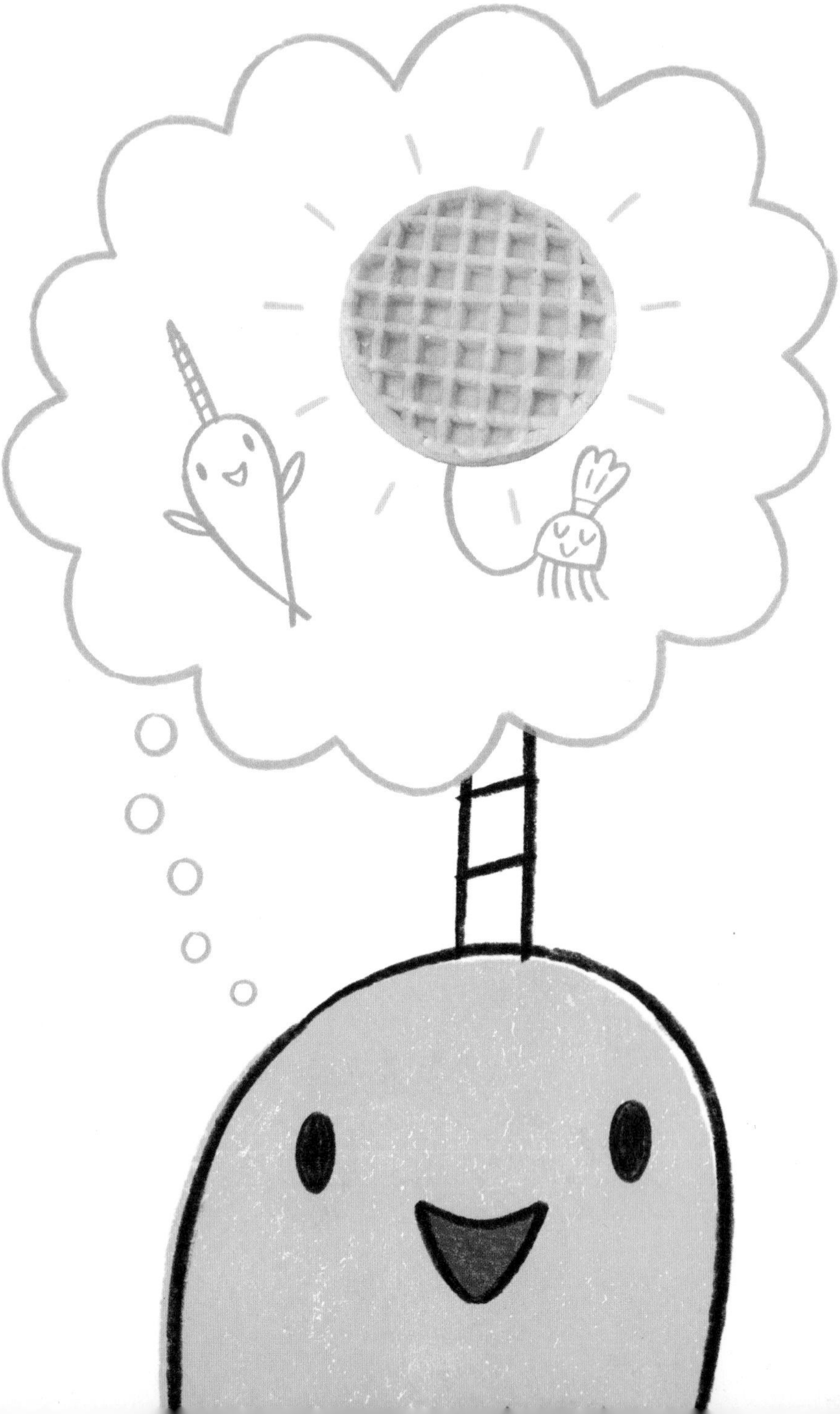

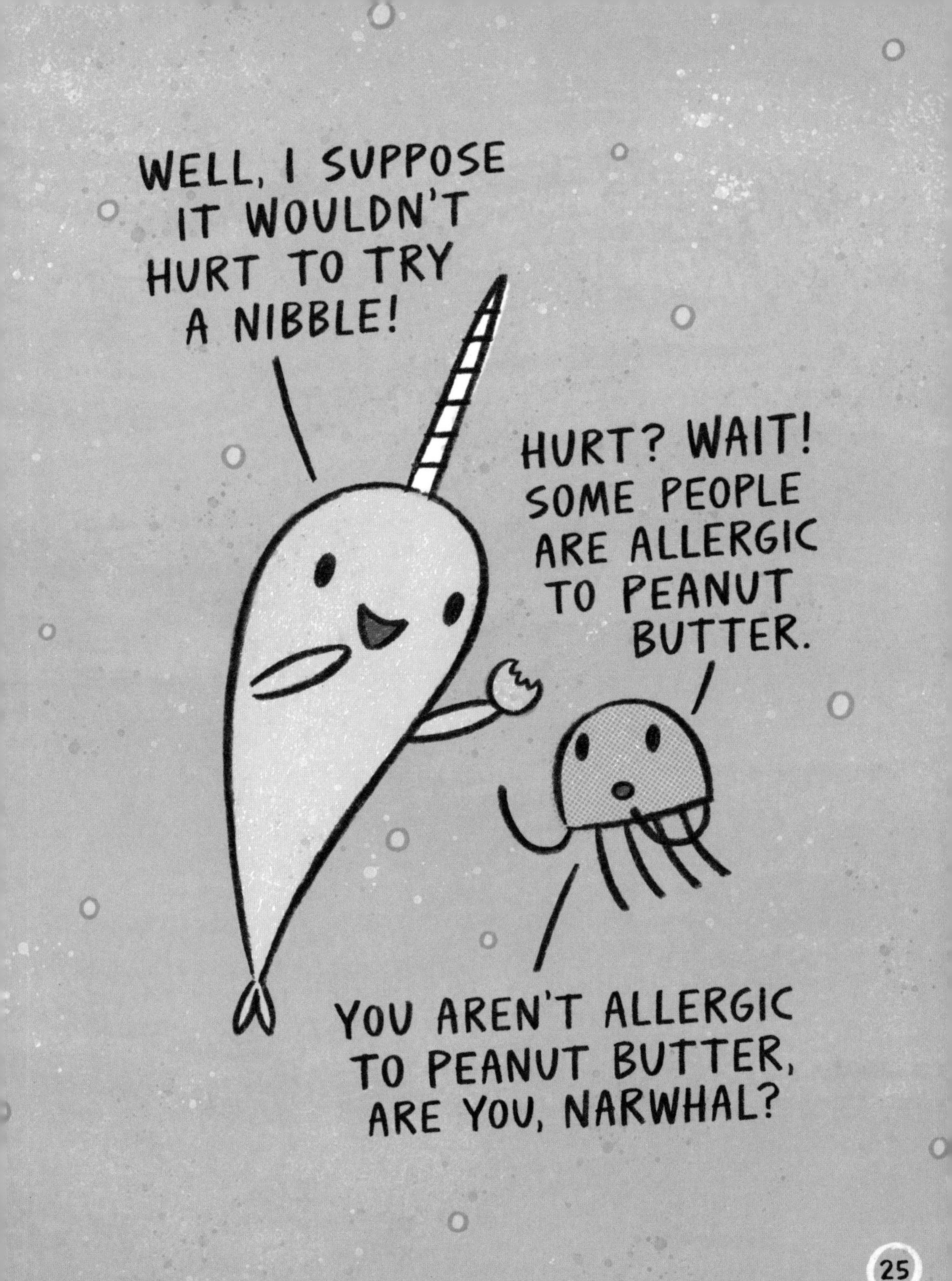
WELL, I SUPPOSE IT WOULDN'T HURT TO TRY A NIBBLE!
HURT? WAIT! SOME PEOPLE ARE ALLERGIC TO PEANUT BUTTER.
YOU AREN'T ALLERGIC TO PEANUT BUTTER, ARE YOU, NARWHAL?

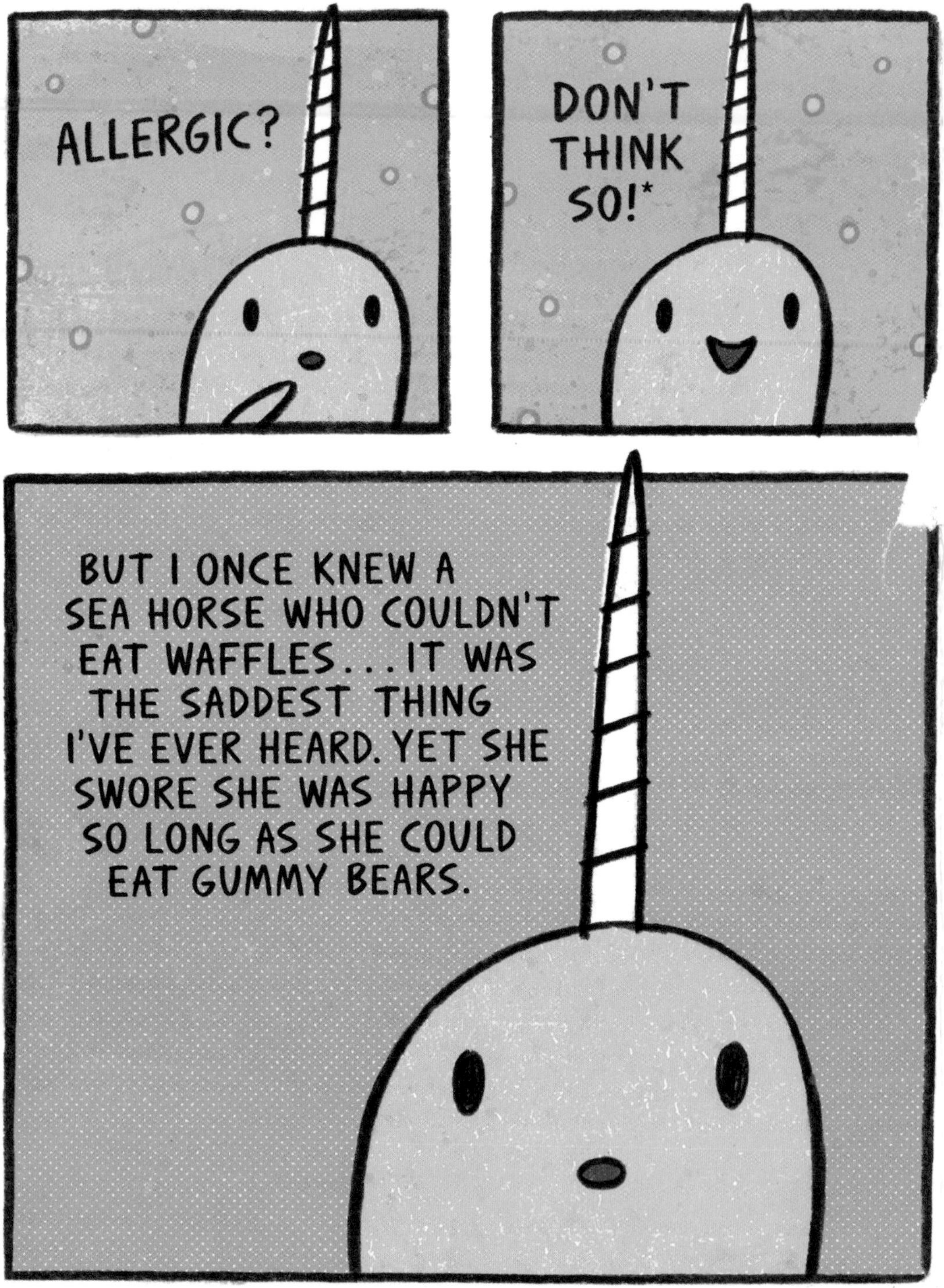
ALLERGIC?
DON'T THINK SO!*
BUT I ONCE KNEW A SEA HORSE WHO COULDN'T EAT WAFFLES...IT WAS THE SADDEST THING I'VE EVER HEARD. YET SHE SWORE SHE WAS HAPPY SO LONG AS SHE COULD EAT GUMMY BEARS.

*THE ALLERGIC AQUATIC ANIMALS AWARENESS ASSOCIATION ADVISES CAUTION WHEN TRYING A COMMON ALLERGEN.

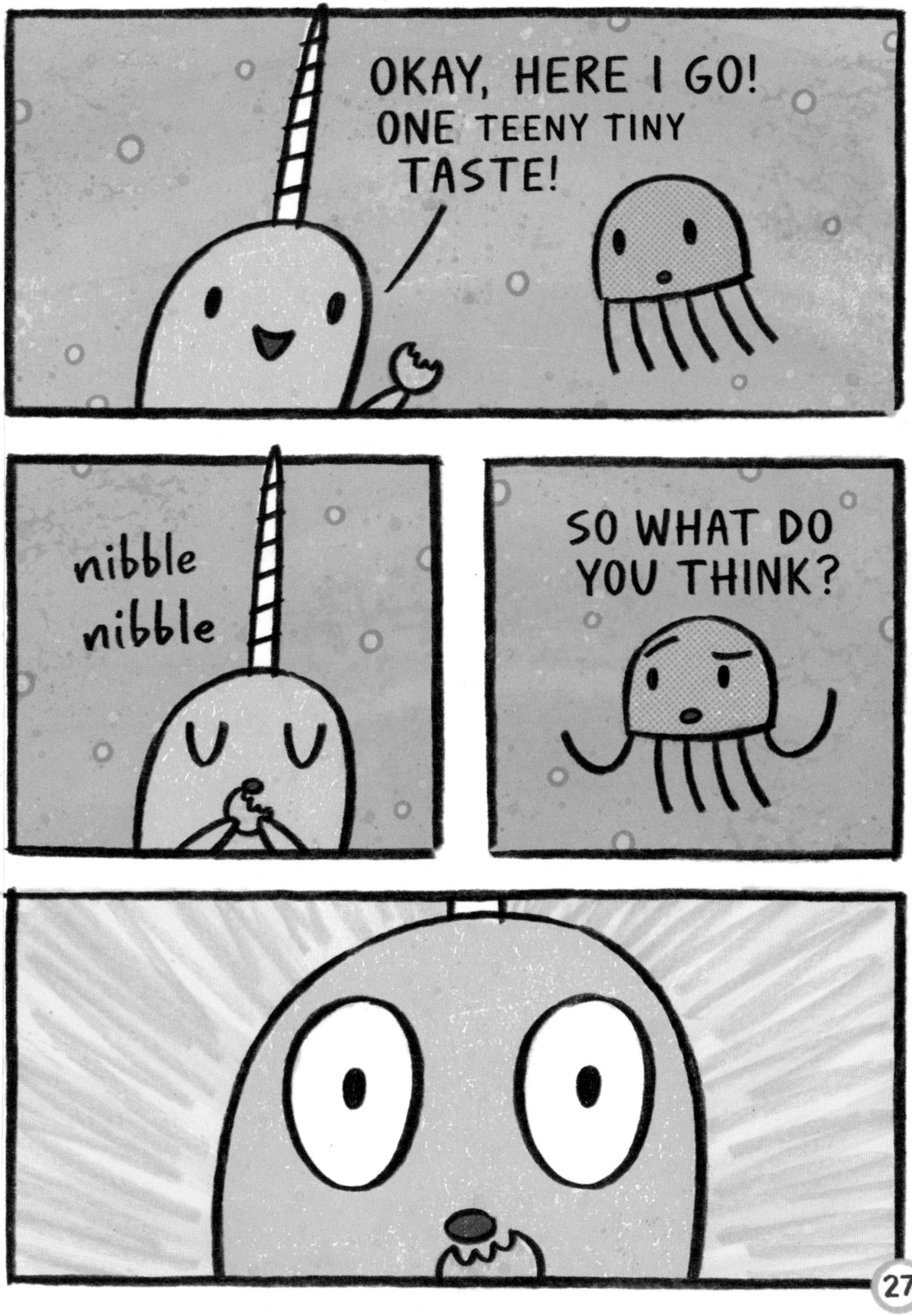
OKAY, HERE I GO! ONE TEENY TINY TASTE!
nibble nibble
SO WHAT DO YOU THINK?

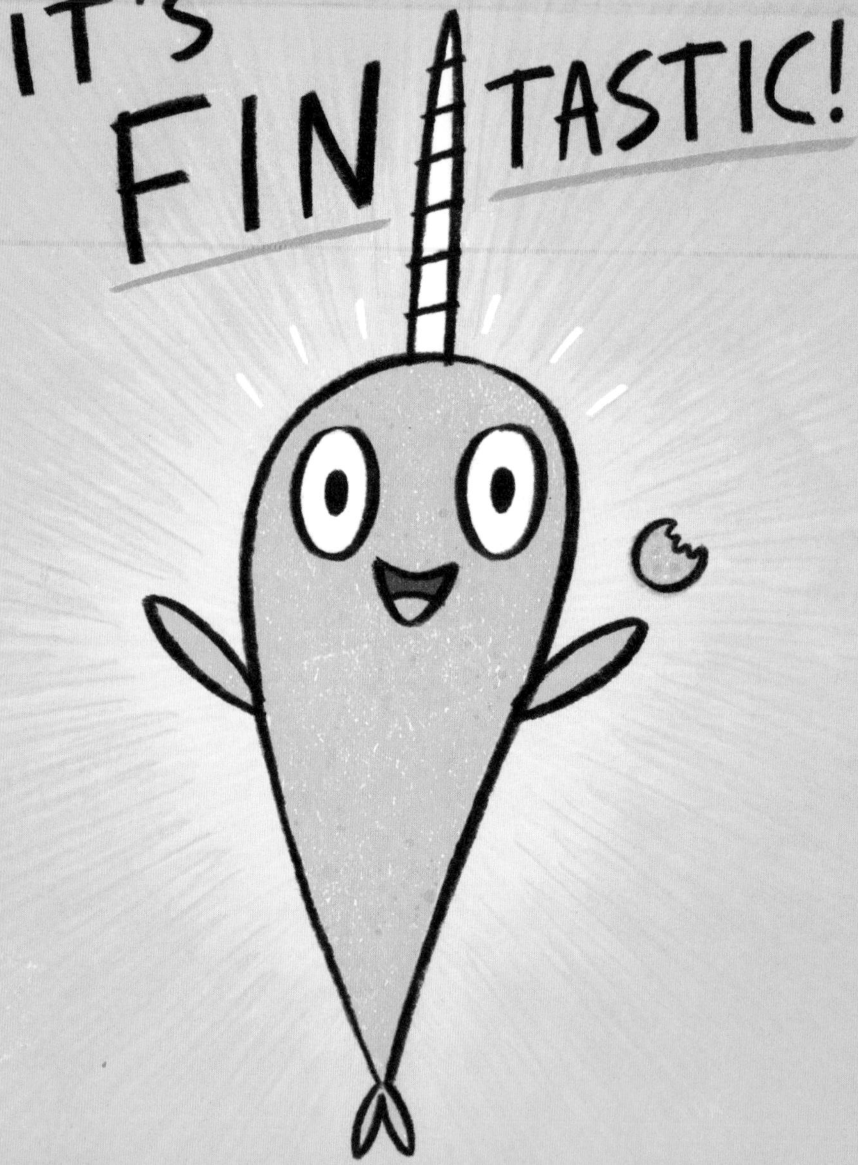
IT'S FIN TASTIC!

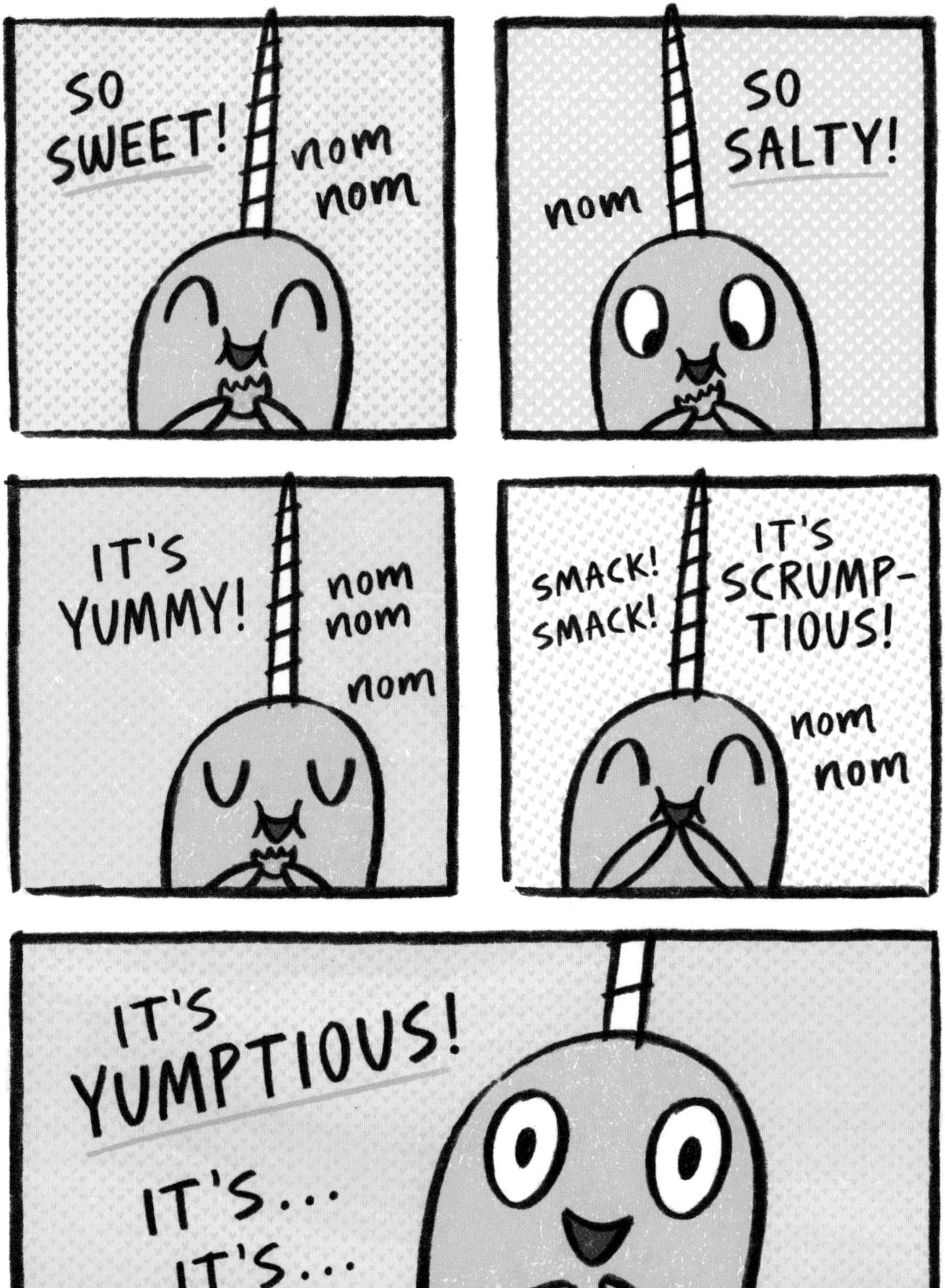
SO SWEET!
nom nom
SO SALTY!
nom
IT'S YUMMY!
nom nom
nom
SMACK! SMACK!
IT'S SCRUMP-TIOUS!
nom nom
IT'S YUMPTIOUS!
IT'S...
IT'S...

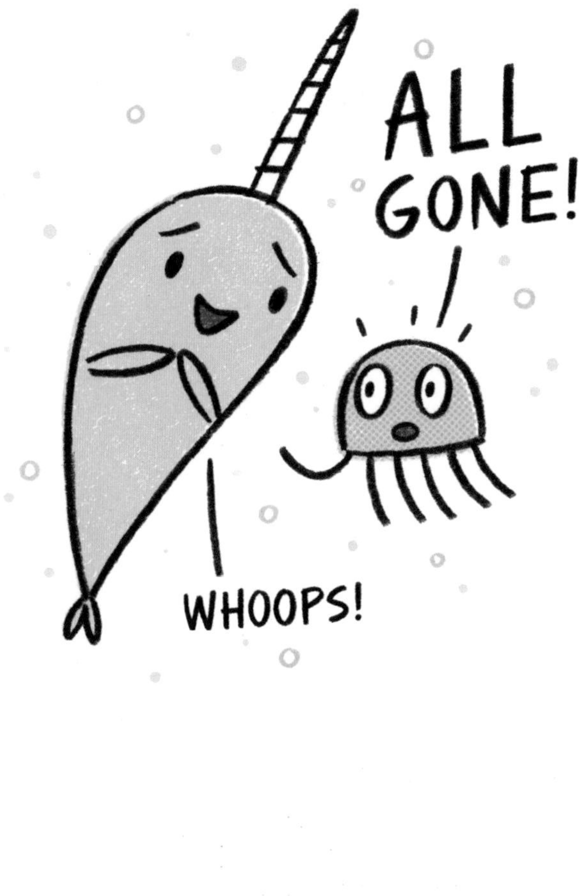
ALL GONE!
WHOOPS!

DELICIOUS FACTS

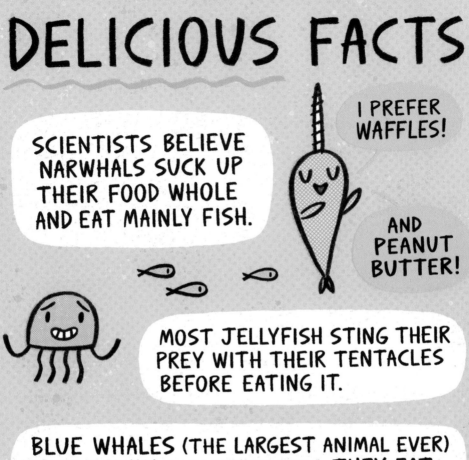

SCIENTISTS BELIEVE NARWHALS SUCK UP THEIR FOOD WHOLE AND EAT MAINLY FISH.

I PREFER WAFFLES!

AND PEANUT BUTTER!

MOST JELLYFISH STING THEIR PREY WITH THEIR TENTACLES BEFORE EATING IT.

BLUE WHALES (THE LARGEST ANIMAL EVER) EAT MAINLY TINY LITTLE KRILL. THEY EAT OODLES OF THEM. AS MANY AS 40 MILLION KRILL PER DAY!

YUM!

EEK!

HUMPBACK WHALES WORK TOGETHER TO CREATE COMPLEX BUBBLE NETS TO CORRAL FISH TO EAT.

SEA CUCUMBERS EAT ALL SORTS OF THINGS, INCLUDING POOP.

TIGER SHARKS ARE OFTEN REFERRED TO AS "THE TRASH CANS OF THE SEA" BECAUSE THEY WILL EAT JUST ABOUT ANYTHING, FROM PIGS TO TIRES TO EXPLOSIVES.

AHOY, PEANUT BUTTER?

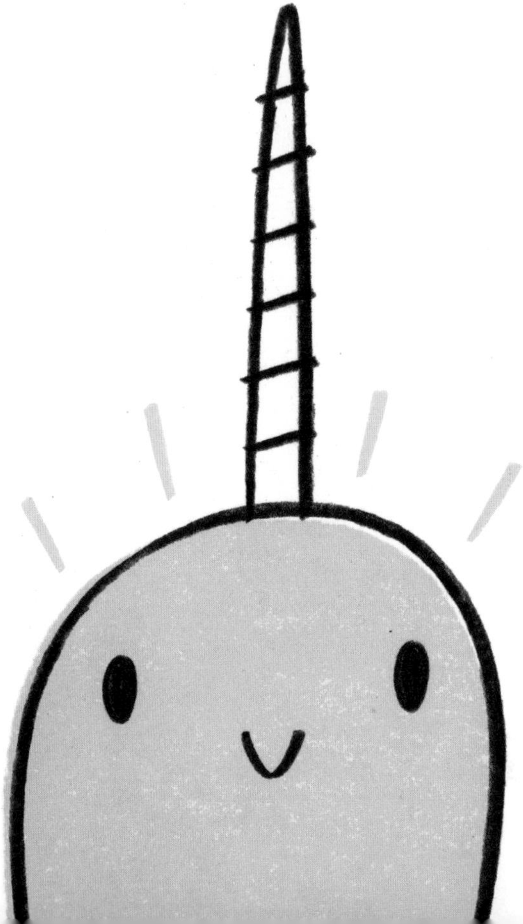

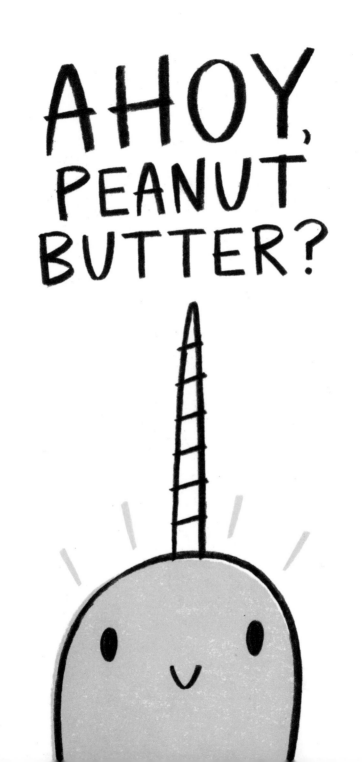

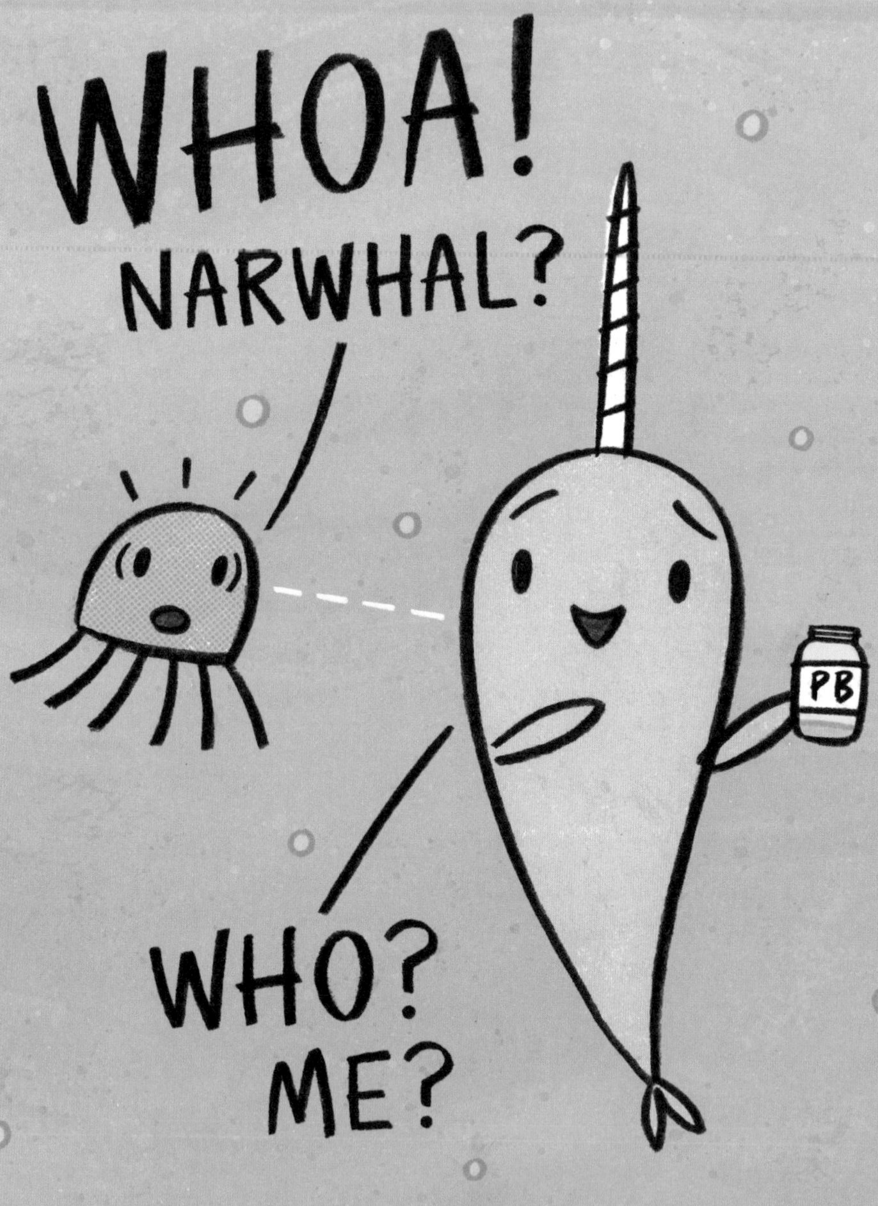
WHOA! NARWHAL?
PB
WHO? ME?

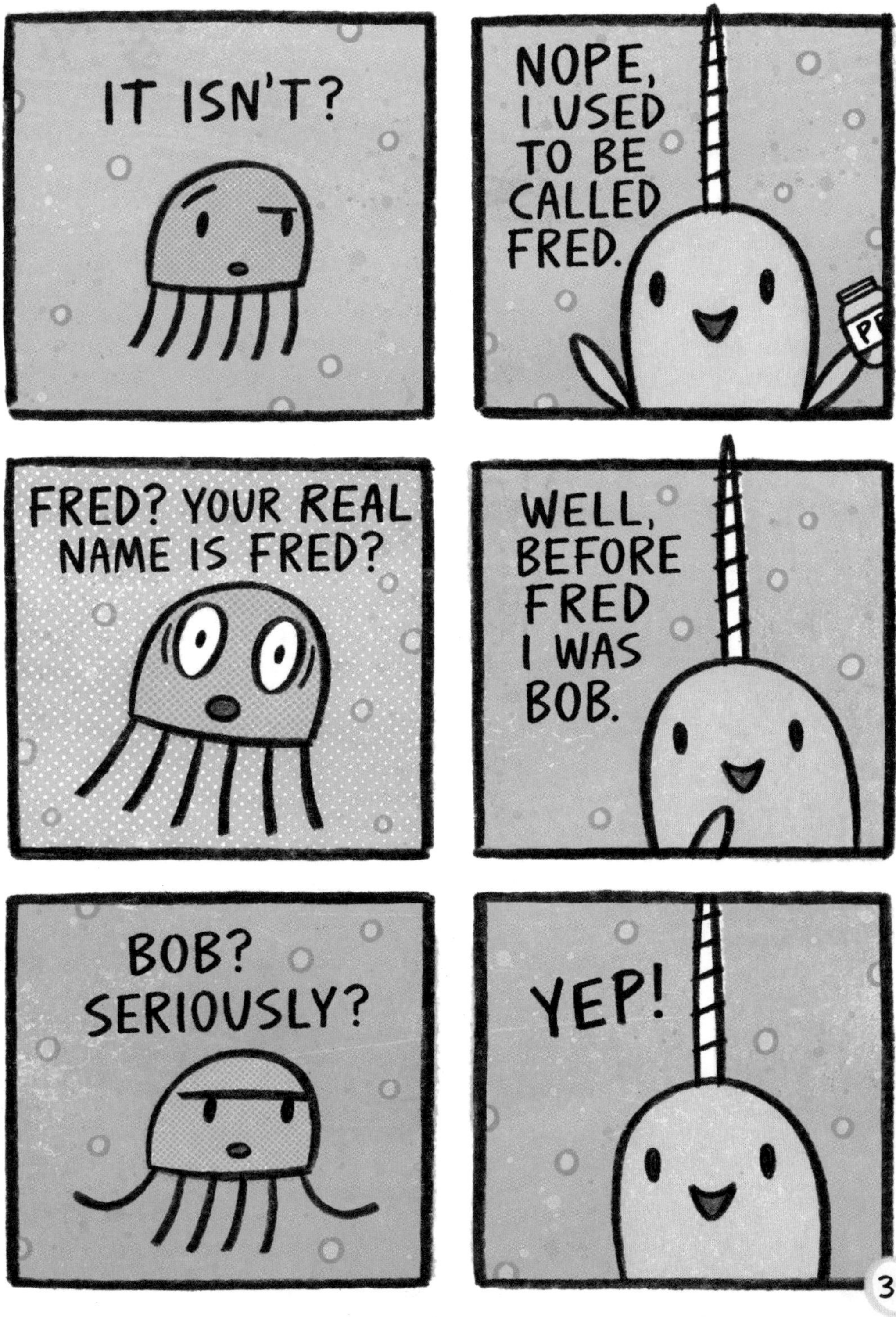
IT ISN'T?
NOPE, I USED TO BE CALLED FRED.
FRED? YOUR REAL NAME IS FRED?
WELL, BEFORE FRED I WAS BOB.
BOB? SERIOUSLY?
YEP!

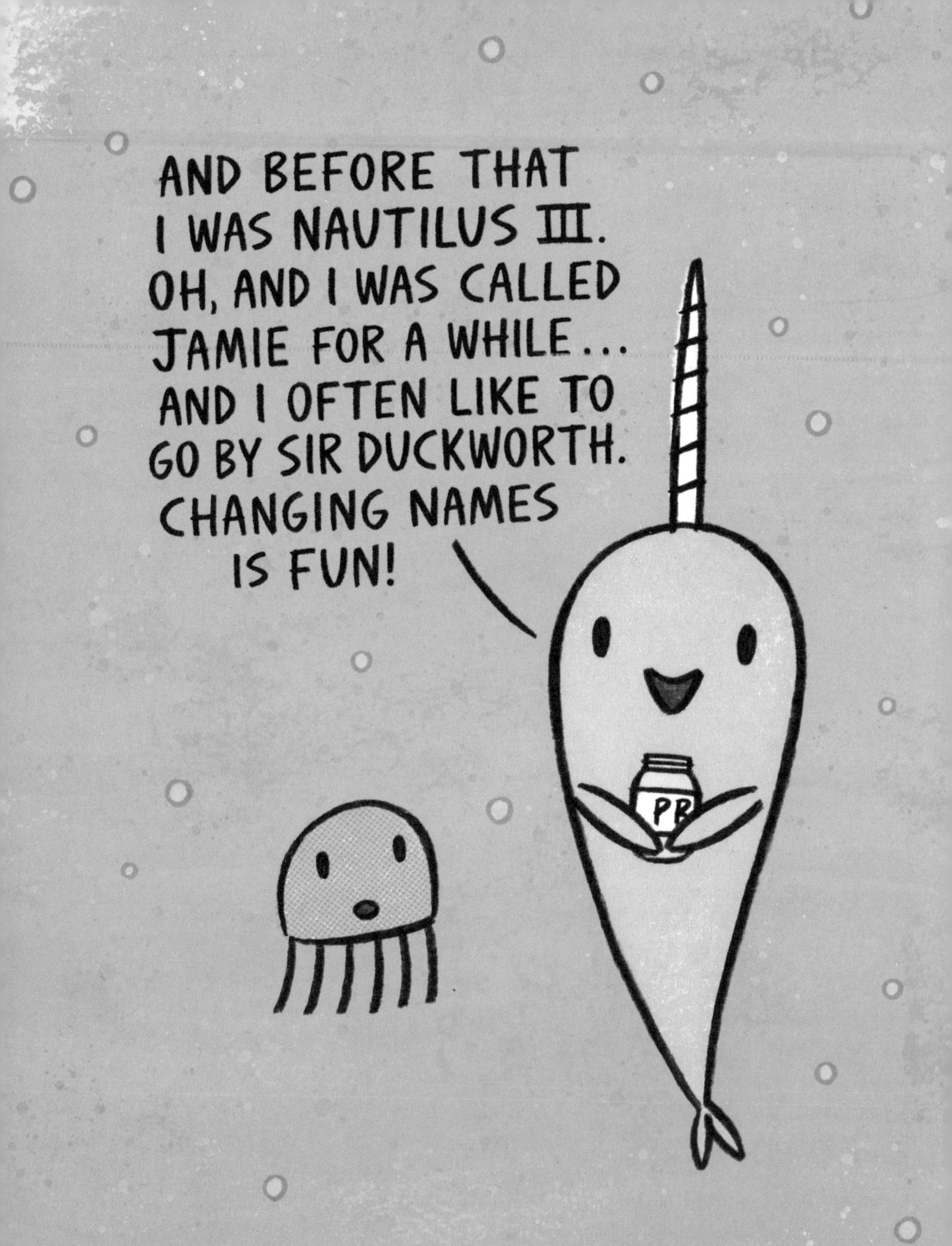
AND BEFORE THAT I WAS NAUTILUS III. OH, AND I WAS CALLED JAMIE FOR A WHILE... AND I OFTEN LIKE TO GO BY SIR DUCKWORTH. CHANGING NAMES IS FUN!

UGH! LOOK, PEANUT BUTTER OR **NARWHAL** OR **FRED** OR WHATEVER YOU ARE CALLING YOURSELF... DON'T YOU THINK YOU'RE TAKING THIS PEANUT BUTTER THING A BIT TOO FAR?

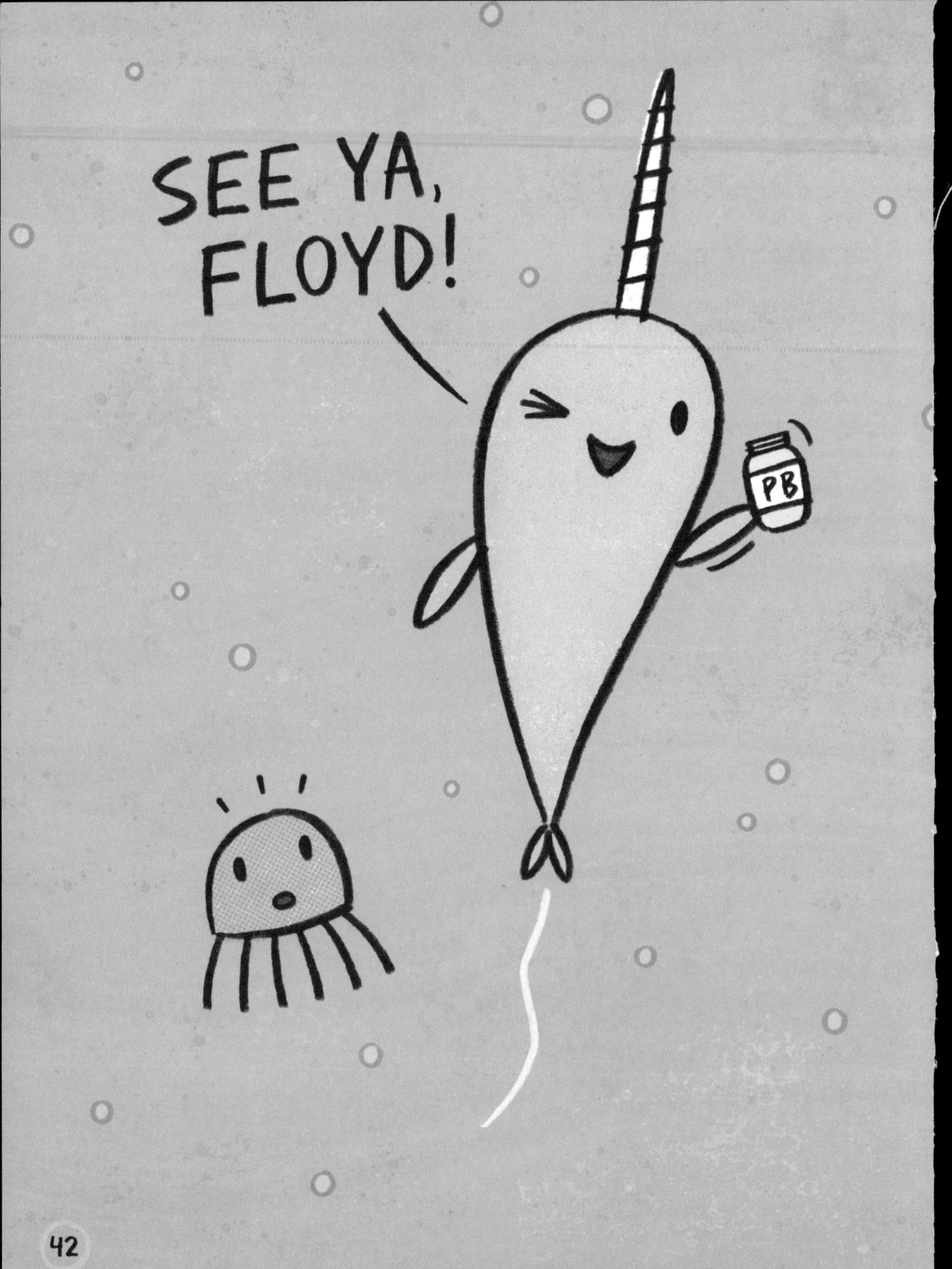
SEE YA, FLOYD!
PB

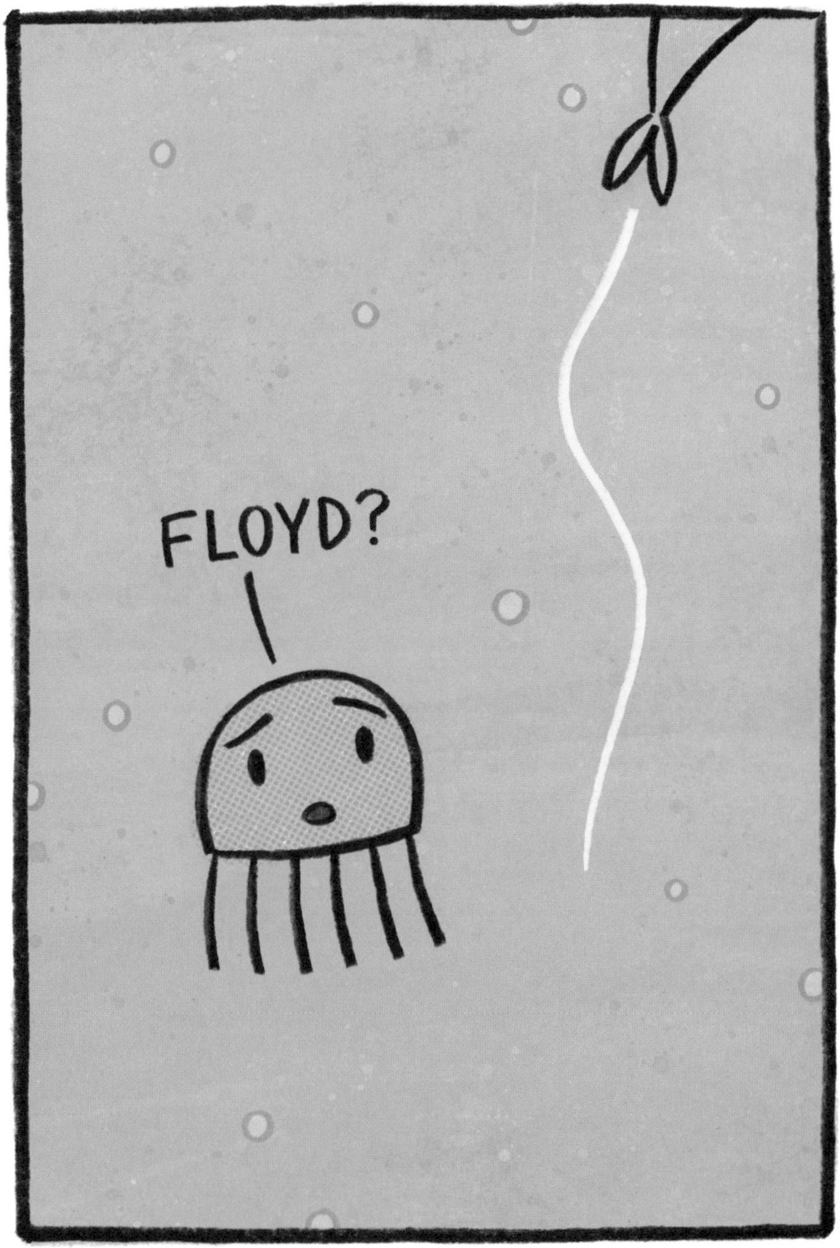
FLOYD?

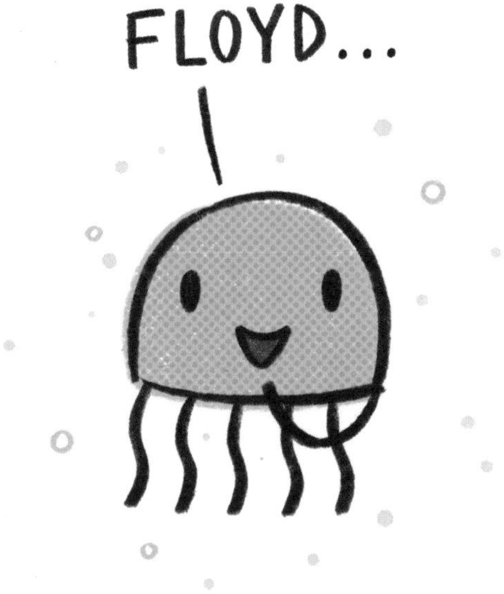
FLOYD...

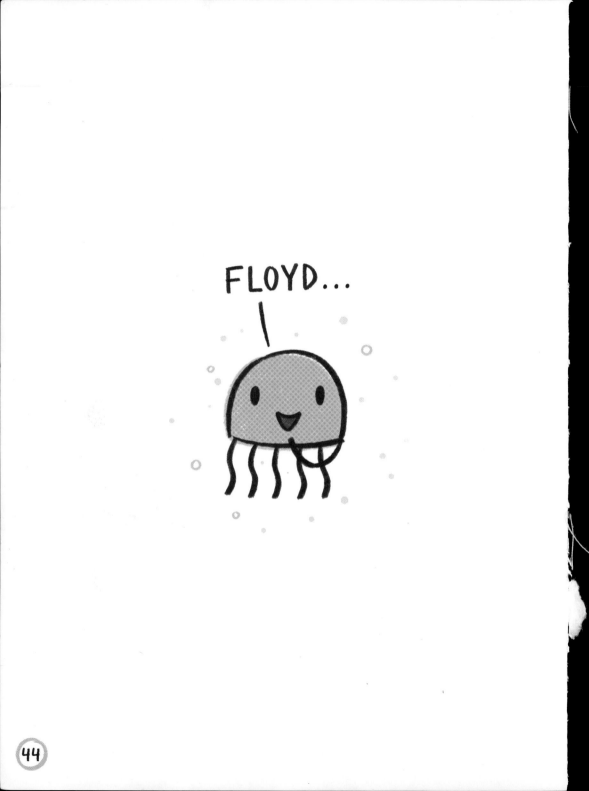

SUPER WAFFLE
AND STRAWBERRY SIDEKICK
VS. PB&J

Peanut Butter   Floyd
by ~~Narwhal~~ and ~~Jelly~~

SUPER WAFFLE AND STRAWBERRY SIDEKICK HAVE BEATEN ANGRY ROBOTS AND VILLAINOUS BLOBS, SO THIS PICKLE WILL BE A PIECE OF CAKE ... PIECE OF PICKLE?

45

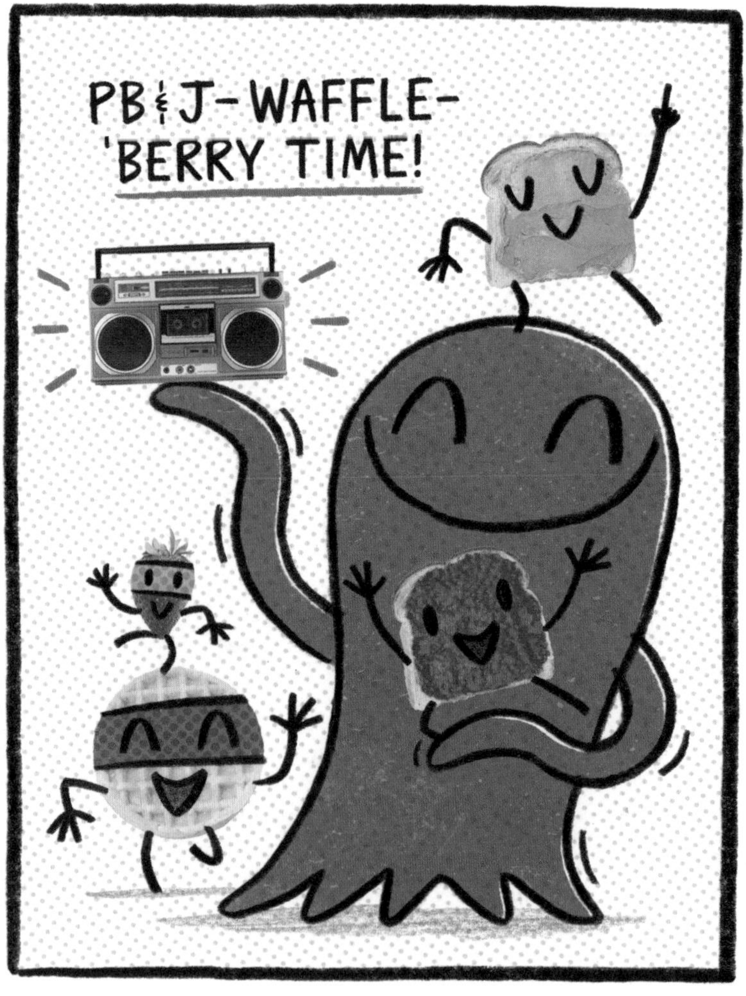
PB & J-WAFFLE-'BERRY TIME!

PEANUT

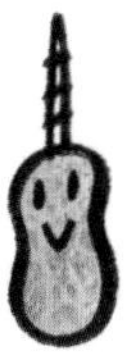

A.K.A. mini
NARWHAL

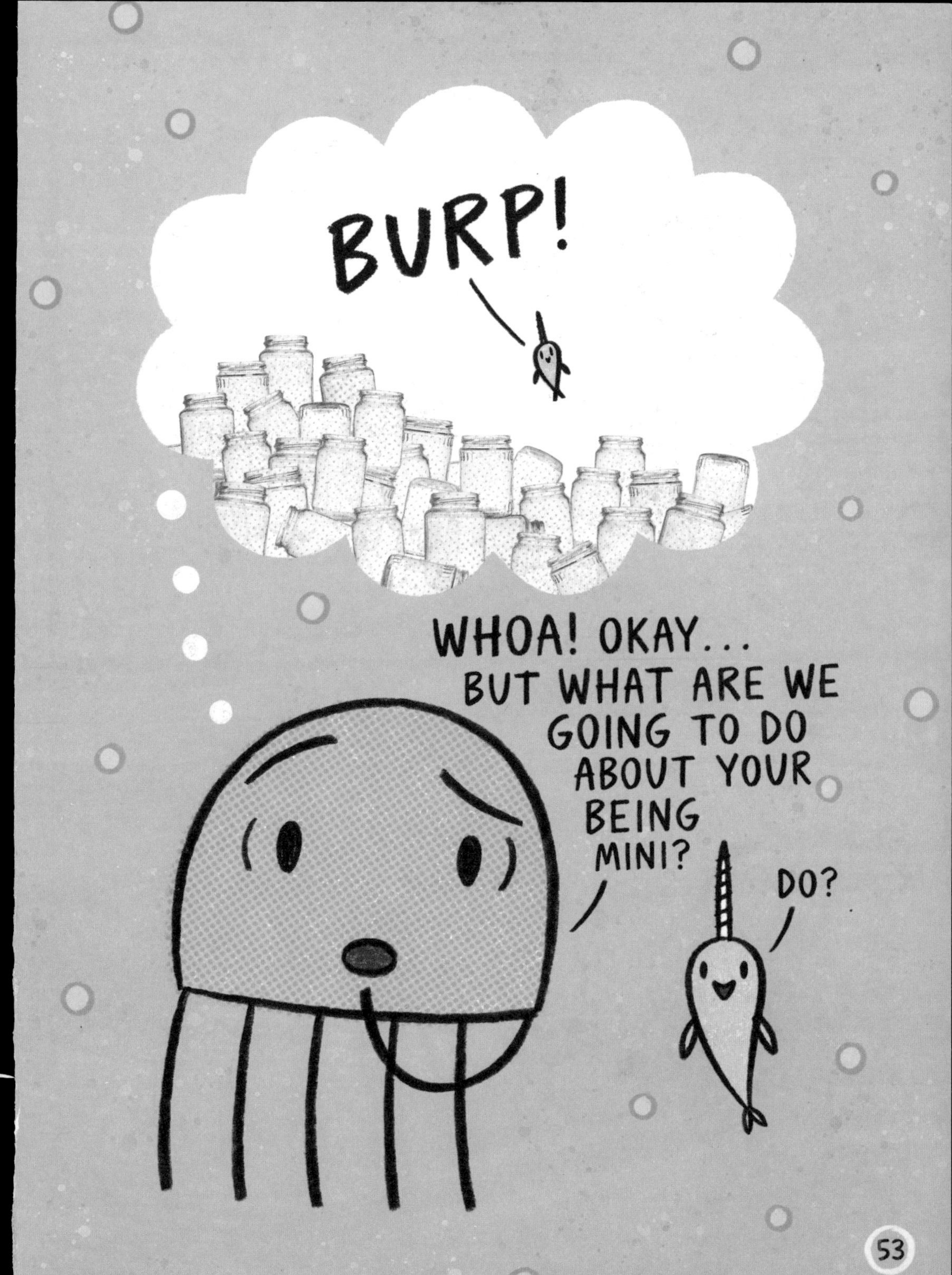
BURP!
WHOA! OKAY... BUT WHAT ARE WE GOING TO DO ABOUT YOUR BEING MINI?
DO?

YES! AREN'T YOU WORRIED YOU'LL BE PEANUT-SIZED FOREVER?
NOT REALLY!

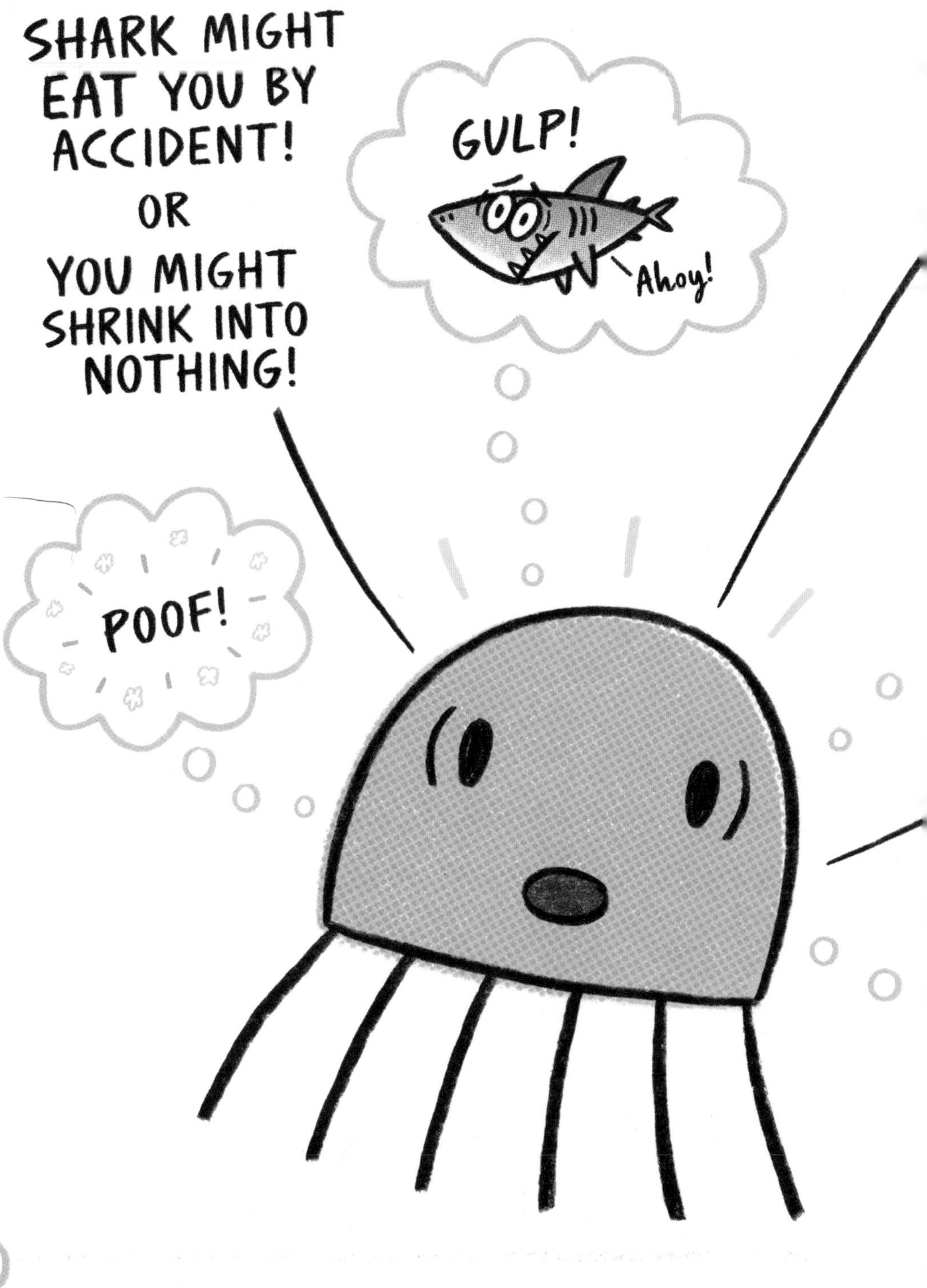
SHARK MIGHT EAT YOU BY ACCIDENT!
OR
YOU MIGHT SHRINK INTO NOTHING!
GULP!
Ahoy!
POOF!

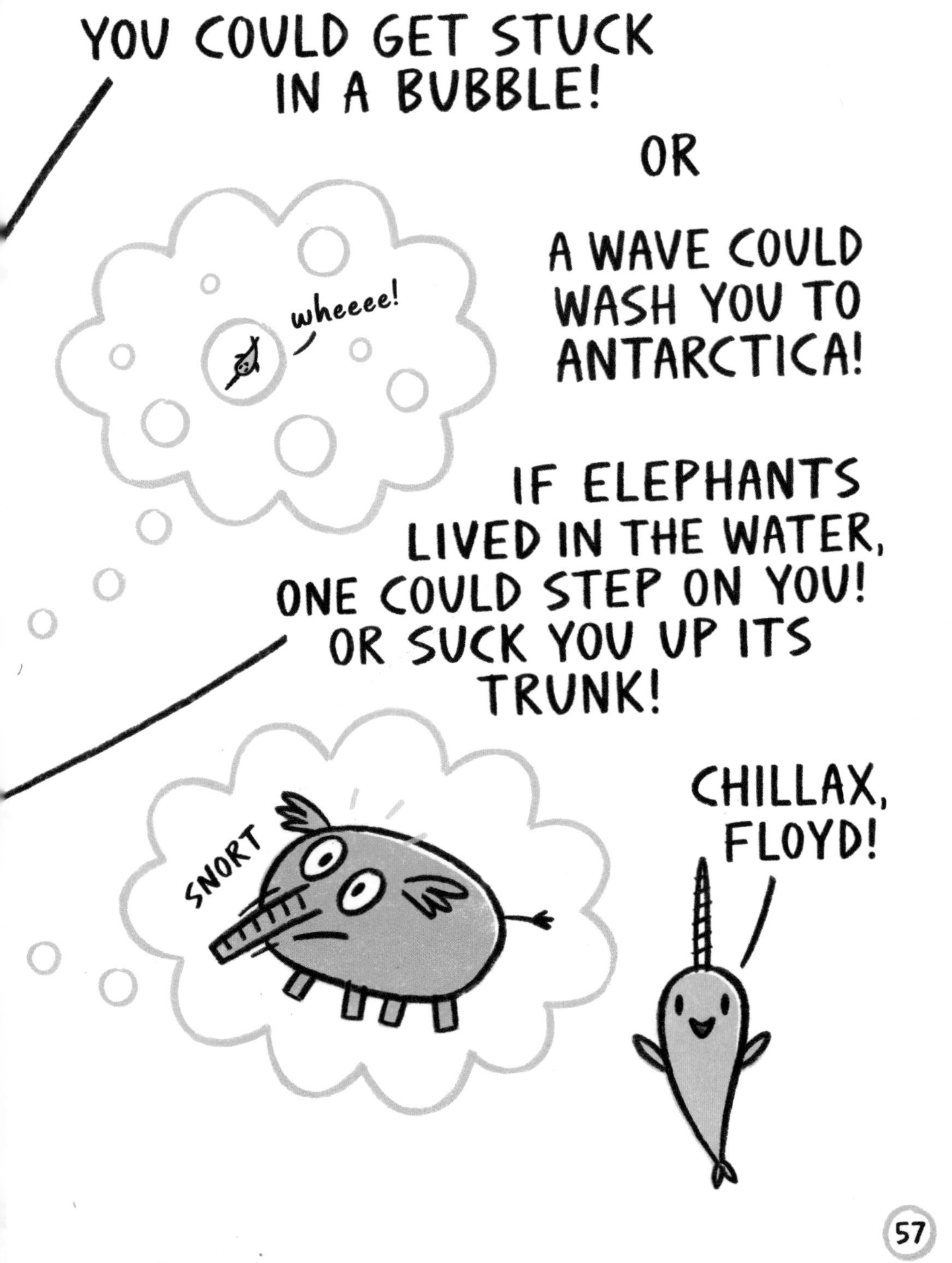
YOU COULD GET STUCK IN A BUBBLE!
OR
wheeee!
A WAVE COULD WASH YOU TO ANTARCTICA!
IF ELEPHANTS LIVED IN THE WATER, ONE COULD STEP ON YOU! OR SUCK YOU UP ITS TRUNK!
SNORT
CHILLAX, FLOYD!

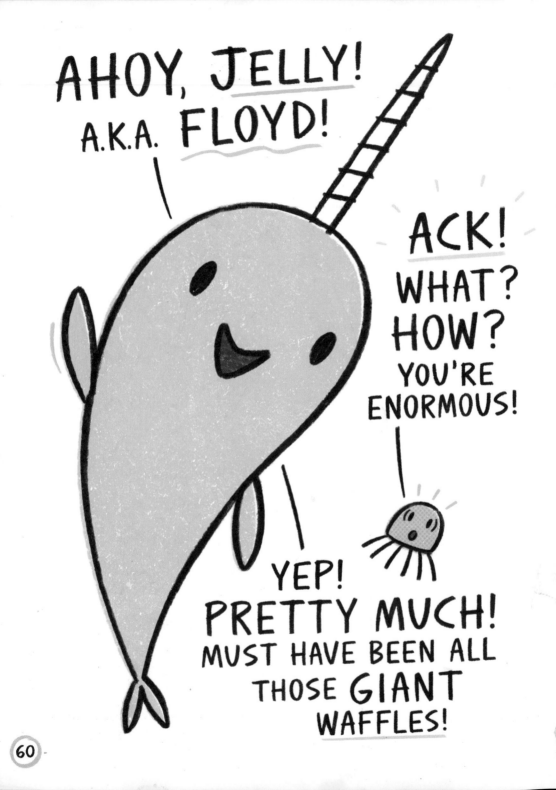

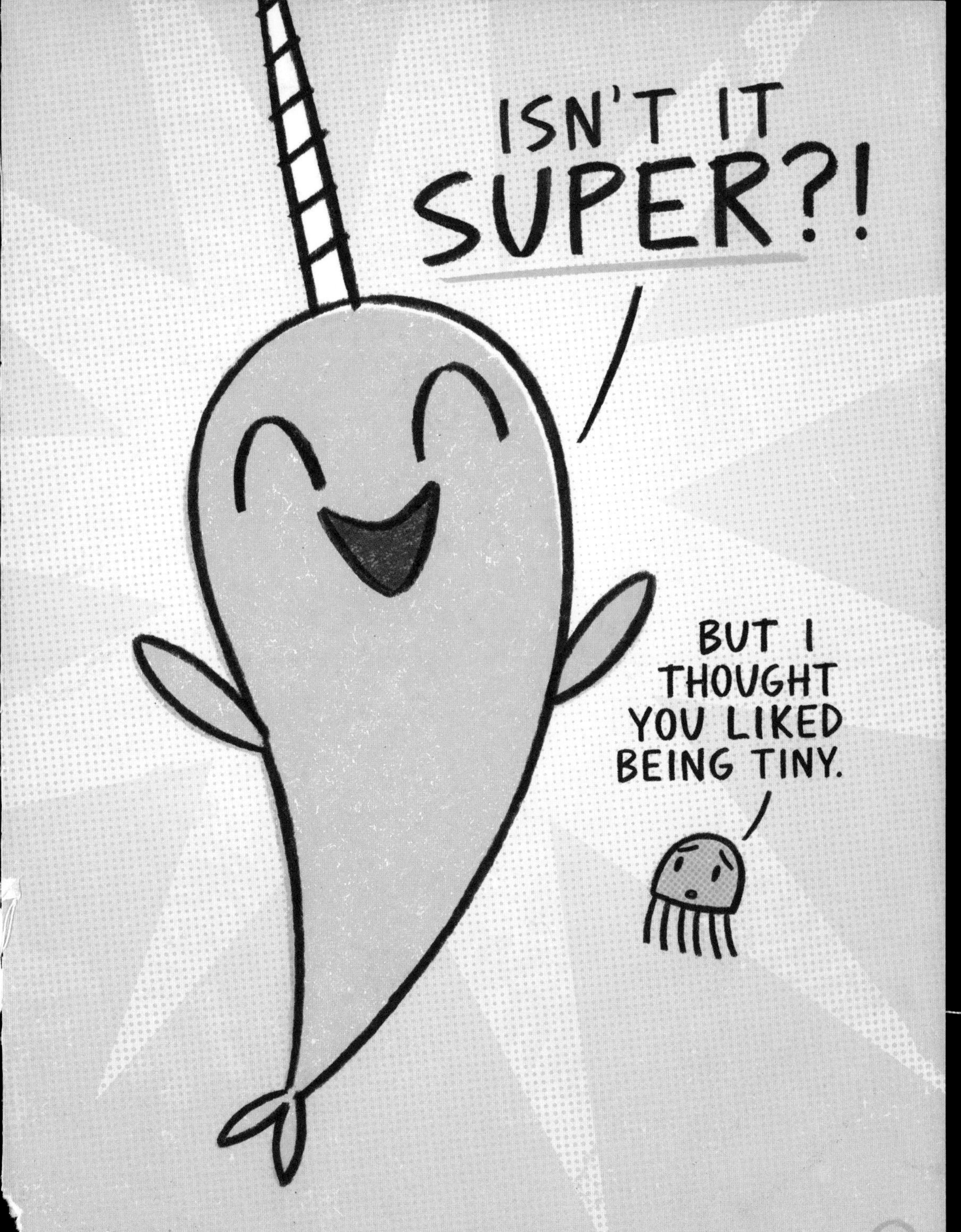
ISN'T IT SUPER?!
BUT I THOUGHT YOU LIKED BEING TINY.

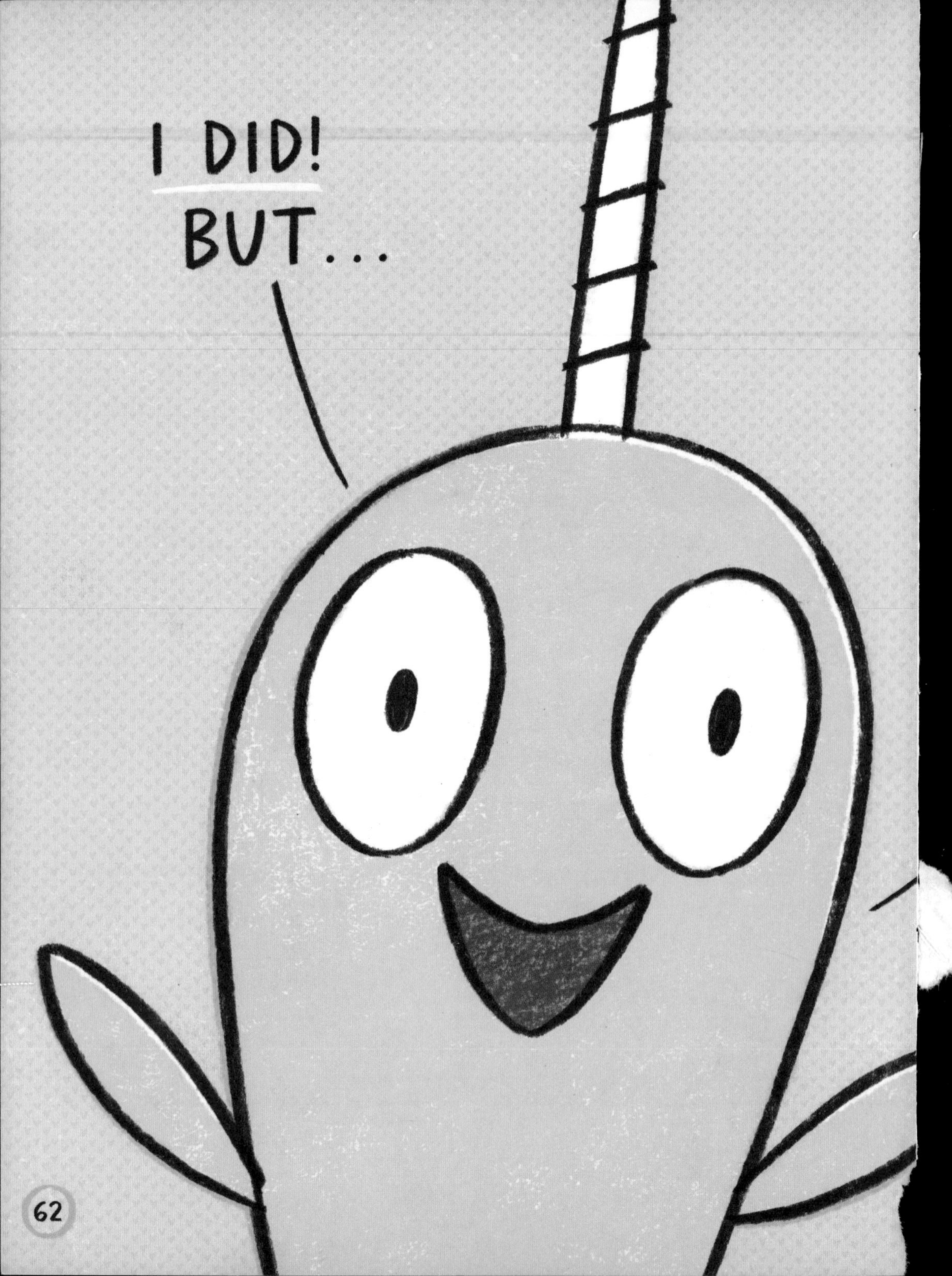
I DID! BUT...

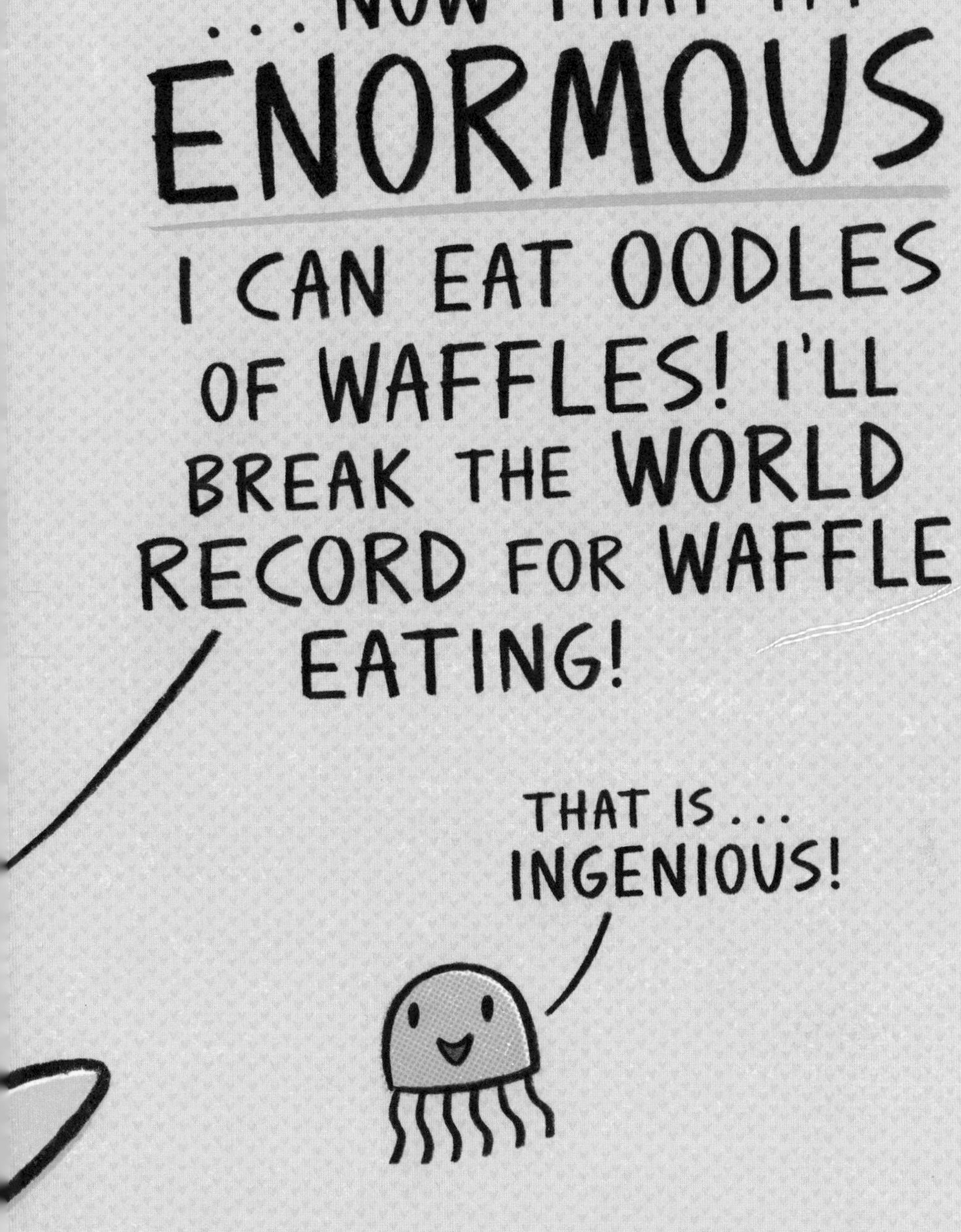
...NOW THAT I'M ENORMOUS I CAN EAT OODLES OF WAFFLES! I'LL BREAK THE WORLD RECORD FOR WAFFLE EATING!
THAT IS... INGENIOUS!